RESOLUTE

VENGEANCE AND VAMPIRES BOOK THREE

ALICIA RADES

Published by Crystallite Publishing LLC.
Produced in the United States of America.
Edited by Megan Linski.
Cover design by KnesArt.

For the ones still searching for themselves.

VENN

Rachel Collins didn't know how amazing she was. It wasn't just that she was beautiful. I mean, she was. Her smile made my heart beat in an unnatural rhythm. At first, I thought there was something wrong with me, but Ryland assured me *That's love, bro.*

Rae's pale skin was flawlessly beautiful, and I constantly had to restrain myself from running my fingers through her sleek black hair just to feel how soft it was. Every now and then, I caught my eyes roaming over her trim figure. I didn't want to be *that* guy, but I couldn't help it. It was like she'd been carved from magic.

But all of that was superficial. She could look like anything and I'd still want to be with her. I mean, the girl killed vampires on the daily for fun. She was totally badass, and to be honest, I was a little jealous of her skills.

She was serious most of the time, but every so often, she'd make a snarky comment that made me laugh, or her eyes would twinkle when she was reminded of her family, and I knew—this girl was made for me.

I couldn't take my eyes off her. I sat on the couch in Genevieve's lake house half an hour outside of Nocton. Genevieve had offered for us to stay here while we all healed and she worked on finding a lead on Matias, who had escaped from our grasp with a very powerful artifact only days ago. Genevieve was a dark witch and a selfish one. I knew she'd drop the offer for a roof over our heads the second she was finished with us, but we were all involved in this now. We were in it with her until the Artifact was finally destroyed.

The cabin was the size of our house, with a high ceiling that stretched to the second level. There were two bedrooms and a bathroom up there, and a loft that overlooked the common area. The kitchen sat open to the living room, so I could easily see everyone else from where I sat. The entire cabin was bathed in natural textures and earthy tones, from the thick wooden beams above our heads to the marble countertop and stone fireplace.

Across the cabin, Rae and Ryland sat opposite each other at the dining room table. Their hands locked together, each of them resting an elbow on the table in an arm wrestle. Neither of them was making any headway to either side. Ryland's eyebrows knitted together. He was still pissed since he found out Rae was Elizabeth Martin in a past life, the witch who'd created the vampire curse. No doubt he'd challenged her to an arm wrestle to relieve some of his frustrations and show her up. And she gladly accepted, knowing he drastically underestimated her.

Ryland's face twisted in concentration. The dude was trying damn hard, which was hilarious considering he was the size of a school bus and Rae looked like a pixie compared to him.

I guess that was what happened when you dealt with

shifter magic. Some shifters were naturally stronger than others, no matter what animal they shifted into. I wondered if Rae's strength had anything to do with the fact that she was a witch, like she was stronger because she had more magic running through her veins or something.

Her lips twisted up into a sly smile. God, I swear the twitch of those perfect lips stopped my heart right there. The book I'd been flipping through fell from my fingertips and onto the floor.

No one noticed my blatant gaping. Rae and Ryland were too preoccupied with wrestling one another, and Fiona and Teagan kept close watch, hooting and hollering for Rae. Sondra was nowhere to be seen, since she was in the other room on the phone.

"Go, go, go!" Fiona shouted, pounding her fist on the table in delight.

"You've got this, Rae," Teagan cheered.

"Seriously, babe?" Ryland asked flatly.

Teagan shrugged. "She's kicking your ass. I officially love her."

Me, too. I just didn't know how to tell her.

"Aww," Rae replied to Teagan. "That's sweet. What do you say, Ryland? Winner gets Teagan?"

"Done," Teagan agreed without so much as a glance toward her boyfriend.

"*Babe!*" Ryland objected. The muscles in his arms rippled as he tried harder to push Rae's arm to the table.

The three girls burst into a fit of laughter. Just seeing Rae smile like that sent tingles up and down my body.

I couldn't deny it. I was head over heels for this girl. She was smart... funny... and she wanted *me*. Not only that, but she treated me like a real human being. Before Sondra rescued me from Maliya's nest, most people in my life had treated me like they owned me. It took me a long time to realize not everyone was like that.

Guilt knotted in the pit of my stomach. Rae sure didn't treat me like a piece of property, but I'd been horrible to her these past few days. I thought girls were supposed to like it when guys acted all protective or whatever, but Rae wasn't like most girls. If she set her mind to something, she was going after it one way or another. Lately, she'd been talking about going after Valkas.

Yes, *that* Valkas, the original vampire—the guy who orchestrated the kidnappings and killings of thousands of people in the last decade. He was heartless, ruthless... the worst kind of being imaginable.

Of course, that was exactly Rae's cup of tea. The badder they were, the more driven she was to destroy them.

Which would've been fine... under normal circumstances. I'd follow her to the ends of the earth to help her. But things changed when I learned that Rae was the one who created Valkas in a past life. Which meant she was the only one who could destroy him in this life. Every time I thought about it, my throat turned to sandpaper and my chest felt as if a ton of bricks was sitting upon it.

It wasn't that I didn't think Rae could kill Valkas. I mean, it was a long shot, but she was strong and smart. She obviously had a chance if she played her cards right. But I feared what would happen to her if the cards didn't play in her favor. What if Valkas discovered who she was? I couldn't bring myself to picture the horrible things he would do to her if he found out *she* was the one thing who could destroy him.

Unlike other vampires, Valkas couldn't die via a stake to the heart, decapitation, or fire. He was the eye of the storm, and it took the witch who started that storm to end it. If she failed, her fate would be far worse than death. Valkas wouldn't just kill her. If he did, her soul would return in less than a century in another body with the chance to take him out again. Death was hardly the worst thing that could happen to a person. He'd find a way to trap her soul—or destroy it. It was the only way to ensure he could live forever.

I sighed, feeling completely heartbroken as I watched her. She smiled across the table at Ryland. She had no idea what kind of terrors lie ahead if she went through with this. The only reason I hadn't told her why I insisted she didn't go was because I was certain it would only drive her closer to Valkas. If there was ass to kick, she was right there to shove her foot straight up it.

Not only that, but I was selfish as all hell. I knew from the moment I saw her that we were destined to be together. I saw something in her eyes the night we'd met, something that looked so familiar it knocked the wind right out of me. There was an instant connection because we'd already lived a whole lifetime together... and I wanted to live every other lifetime with her, too.

"Surrender!" Rae demanded with a laugh, cutting through my thoughts.

Sweat had broken out on both her and Ryland's heads.

"No," Ryland objected. "I'm not losing to a girl."

Rae scoffed. "You're not winning to one, either."

Fiona doubled over in a fit of laughter. Even I snickered.

Shit, I couldn't let this girl go, not right when I'd found her. I'd waited years for her to show up. I didn't know I was waiting for *her*, of course, but I knew I was waiting for *someone*. I had the sketches from Sondra to prove it. They were tucked in the outer pocket of my duffel bag. I'd pulled them off the wall before our house burned down.

Sondra couldn't exactly tell the future. No witch could without a magical object to assist them. But they could get a sense of where Synchrony was leading you. Sondra knew Synchrony was leading me to Rae long before Rae ever stepped into my life. She'd drawn the sketches to give me hope.

Rae pushed with all her might, making headway. Ryland pushed back, but Rae had already gained the upper hand. He conceded before his hand ever hit the table.

Ryland dropped Rae's hand and crossed his arms. "Okay, I give, but only because I have a bad arm."

He scowled and rubbed his bicep, which wasn't even the arm that had been broken. Besides, he'd undergone enough healing spells that it should've been good as new by now.

Rae shot her fists into the air in victory. My heart danced inside my chest when I saw the overly excited look on her face. Most of the time, she was all business. It was nice to see her beaming for once. And lord, was it beautiful.

Teagan and Fiona both gave Rae a high-five before she stood from her chair and turned to me with a smile.

Slay. The girl effing slayed me. She was perfect.

She caught me staring, and I involuntarily blushed under her gaze. She didn't notice.

Rae wiggled her eyebrows. "Your turn to challenge the beast, Venn."

I sat up straighter and laughed. "Believe me, Ryland and I have had our fair share of show-downs."

Rae smirked. "Me, Venn. I meant *me.*"

I couldn't help but smile. Holy crap, was it a wide smile. I must've looked like I had a fork stuck sideways in my mouth. But that was the way she made me feel, like there was this light inside of me that had been begging to escape my whole life but was shadowed by all the darkness in my past... until she flipped the switch. All that light came pouring out all at once.

"Nah," I said, waving my hand like it was no big deal. "I think you've already crushed enough sets of balls for the night." My gaze flickered to Ryland, who shot daggers my way.

He scoffed and mumbled, "I'm sure she'll be doing more than that later tonight."

I had the sudden urge to punch him.

Rae crossed her arms and stuck out her hip. I wanted to kiss the pout right off those sexy lips of hers.

"I didn't realize this was the freaking patriarchy," Rae teased with a raise of her eyebrow. "They're not going to revoke your man card."

I shrugged. "They might."

Rae crossed the room and grabbed my hand from off the back of the couch. Fire tingled up and down my skin, but the good kind—the warm kind.

"Come *on*..." she begged. "We're just having fun."

How could I deny her of that? It'd been all business since we met, besides the few minor make out sessions that left us *both* wanting more.

I took a deep breath, pretending like I had to think about it. Finally, I stood and followed her over to the table. "Fine."

"*Whip-cha.*" Ryland made a whipping motion through the air.

"Shut up," I grumbled as I pushed him aside so I could take his seat across from Rae.

"Watch out," he warned as he stood. "This girl is stronger than she looks."

My eyes met hers, and I beamed. "I know."

She gazed back at me with challenging eyes, then took my hand, squeezing it tightly. My breath caught in my chest.

"On the mark of three..." Teagan stated. "One... Two... Three!"

Every muscle in my body tensed as I threw all my strength into the arm wrestle. Damn, this girl was strong. Most girls would go flying across the room under my shifter strength. But Rae was nothing like most girls.

Needless to say, she won the arm wrestle, but I was the lucky guy who won a red-hot consolation kiss.

1

The world had a way of raising you up just to slam you into the dirt the second you thought you were safe. I'd learned to roll with the highs and lows, but I also knew that perfection was only temporary. Which meant that the few days I'd had with my new family in Genevieve's lake house were coming to a close.

Venn and I lay beside each other on one of the big couches in front of the fireplace. We barely fit, but he pulled me securely to his chest to keep me close to him. My ear rested just above his heart. The hairs on my arm rose as I listened to the comforting *thump* of his heartbeat and felt the warmth of his breath across the top of my head. The fireplace crackled, and soft voices from the patio drifted in through the screen door with the cool night breeze.

My fingers ran over the back of Venn's hand, examining the skin that'd been sliced open just days ago. There were no signs of injury anymore, and when I pressed down, he made no indication that it bothered him.

I'd tested Ryland's arm earlier, and that was back to normal—though his attitude hadn't improved much. He didn't say anything when Teagan was around to keep him in line, but I caught him throwing death glares my way every now and then. He looked like he wanted to punch me for what I'd done in a past life. And maybe he would've—if he knew I wouldn't smack him right back.

Through the sliding glass doors, I could see Fiona standing next to Teagan, sipping on her soda and staring out across the lake. It was clear her broken leg was healed as well.

It should've been great news, but it only made me feel sick. I told myself I'd stay long enough for everyone to heal. Now that we were all feeling better, I had to go.

I didn't *want* this amazing mini-vacation to end. For the first time in years, I'd felt normal. I cooked breakfast with Teagan and stayed up late talking with Fiona. We all went swimming in the lake and ate popcorn while we watched a dumb slapstick comedy that made me forget—if only for a moment—that I lived in a world of monsters.

And then there was Venn. Every moment with him was like magic. He took my breath away. It didn't matter the circumstances, whether it was the time I caught him staring while we were cleaning up after dinner, or the time he cornered me in the laundry room and we had the most amazing make out session. I was totally smitten by the guy.

Except for one thing. He didn't want me going after Valkas.

And I *had* to. For one, Jenna was on that island with the bastard, and I already knew without a doubt that I was going after her. But now I had the chance to kill Valkas while I was at it? It wasn't an opportunity I could pass up. Not only did it mean eliminating one of the worst terrorist threats in history, but Matias had said that killing Valkas would kill all the other vampires as well.

"What happens to you when I kill Valkas?" I'd asked him.

"I suppose it breaks the spell," he'd replied. *"Once that magic is no longer keeping me alive, I would die—just as would all the other vampires."*

I'd asked Sondra about it while we were sunbathing along the lakeshore a few days ago, and she agreed it made sense. If I broke the curse, all vampires would perish.

This *had* to be done, and I was the only person who could do it. I only wished I could convince Venn to come with me.

"Venn?" I cleared my throat.

"Yeah, Rae?" He let out a long, soothing breath.

Damn it. He was totally relaxed. I wasn't ready to have this fight with him again… but I couldn't keep putting it off. There was work to be done.

"We need to talk about what's happening next."

Venn's whole body tensed. He glanced down at me. "We're going after Matias. We have to destroy the Artifact."

My jaw clenched. "You know he's not the only threat out there. You promised we'd go after my sister."

Venn sat up straight, pulling his arm out from under me. I nearly toppled off the end of the couch, but I quickly righted myself and sat next to him.

Venn raked his fingers through his dark hair. "That was before. You don't understand how dangerous Gregor Island could be, do you?"

I stared back at him with a stone-cold expression. If he thought I didn't understand the dangers of going after Valkas, he seriously underestimated me. But it was because of those dangers that I had to go. No one had heard from the Soulless in two years, which only meant they were planning something... something *big*. And I had to stop them first.

"I know things changed when Matias gave me that dagger," I said, "but I have to go through with it. I couldn't do it in my past lives because I didn't have the dagger used in the spell that created him. Now I have it, so it's the perfect chance to strike."

Venn's fists tightened, and his gaze narrowed at the flickering flames in the fireplace. "Have you ever considered that maybe Matias was lying to you?"

Honestly, the thought had crossed my mind, but Matias sounded genuine. He truly wanted Valkas dead, so why would he give me a fake dagger? Not to mention I saw the same dagger in a vision—a memory.

"Matias could be working for Valkas," Venn pointed out.

My brow furrowed. "That makes no sense."

"It could be a trap to lure you to Gregor Island."

"Again, that doesn't make sense," I said. "I was already headed there anyway."

Venn's lips tightened, but he didn't respond.

"You know you can't talk me out of this, right?" I asked. "The only question is, are you—or anyone else—going to come with me?"

Venn finally lifted his gaze to mine, but he completely ignored the question. "You can't even go after him without the dagger, and Genevieve has it."

I crossed my arms. "So I'll get it from her. Just remind me again why we trusted her with it?"

Venn took a long breath. "So you wouldn't do anything stupid."

I stood. As much as I adored Venn, he was starting to get on my nerves. Was that supposed to happen with soulmates?

The thought frustrated me even more. "This isn't stupid! This is what I'm supposed to do."

"You aren't *supposed* to do anything!" Venn shot to his feet beside me. He stole a quick glance at the patio doors. Fiona caught his eye but turned back to the lake a second later.

"But I *should*," I said in a softer tone. "The vampire curse is my fault. I have to be the one to stop it."

"It's *not* your fault, though," he argued. "You're different from the girl who created Valkas."

"Different how?" I challenged. "It was my soul. Maybe I was a different person at the time, but that doesn't matter. What matters now is that I'm the only one who can stop it. The laws and blood banks have only slowed the vampires down. They haven't stopped them. They're still out there murdering people and kidnapping them as blood slaves. They have no compassion or remorse and will do anything to serve their own purpose. Wouldn't you do something about that if you could?"

"Yes," he said, "but we have to stop Matias first. If he uses the Artifact before you get to Valkas, you'll lose your powers. You won't be able to defend yourself against Valkas. You said yourself that the Artifact doesn't work on vampires. You'll be up against him and his vampire strength without any powers of your own."

"That's exactly why I have to go. I'll never stand up to Valkas if I lose my magic. What if we fail and Matias uses the Artifact and blocks everyone's magic? I have to get to Gregor Island, kill Valkas, and find my sister all before Matias strikes."

"Look, we won't fail. Valkas will be there when we get back."

"Will he?" I questioned. "What if the Soulless make a move

before we get to Matias? What if this is my only chance? If I kill Valkas, we won't have to worry about Matias."

"And what about his successor?" Venn pointed out.

"You're asking me to sign your death certificate," I'd said to Matias. *"Why would you want that? What about your plan to cure the world?"*

"Vampirism may seem like a blessing," Matias had said. *"I could do so much with my immortality. But there are far more terrible things about it. The constant bloodlust. The emotional disconnect... Vampirism is truly a curse. Once I'm free of the curse, my successor will take my place and carry out my plan."*

"What if his successor is easier to beat?" I asked. "We could kill the vampires, then go after the Artifact."

"And what if his successor is worse?" Venn asked softly.

The room went quiet. It appeared we'd reached an impasse. He reached out to pull me into his arms, and I relaxed into his embrace, inhaling his sweet scent. My whole body shivered beneath his touch. There was no way in hell I'd ever want to abandon these strong, protective arms and the comforting smell of home. If he would just come with me...

Venn drew away slightly, and I tilted my head up to meet his dark brown eyes. His gaze flickered down to my lips, and my mouth went dry. Heaven help me. If he was going to kiss me again, I didn't know if I would ever make it to Gregor Island without him.

"Rae," he whispered, his eyes glistening. "I know danger is your thing, but this is too risky. What if Valkas finds out who you are?"

"He won't," I said with certainty. "I'll never give him the chance."

Venn sighed, still holding my gaze. "I know you think that,

but—" His voice cracked, and he wrapped his arms around me tighter.

I laid my head on his chest, basking in the warmth of his embrace. Tears pricked at my eyes, and I cleared my throat. "This is a pointless argument, Venn. I know you think you can talk me out of it, but like you said, danger is my thing."

Venn paused a beat before speaking. "That's what I was afraid of."

"Besides," I said like it was no big deal, "if I don't get him this time, I'll come back in a few years and get another chance. You'll be drawn to me and recognize me and can tell me all about it."

Venn went rigid. "Rae, I don't think you understand—"

A door banged open down the hall, and Sondra rushed into the living room. "Get everyone in here. I just got a lead on where Matias is staying."

Venn's arms dropped from around me, and cold air rushed in to take his place. "How soon?"

"I'm still waiting for full details," Sondra said, "but we need to start packing. By the time dawn breaks, we're going after him."

There was no talking any sense into Venn. And I thought *I* was supposed to be the stubborn one. Which only left one option. I was doing this without him.

"Venn is going to be beyond pissed," Fiona said when I told her.

We were in the guest room we shared, packing up our stuff. I had all my belongings back since Genevieve had taken them from the apartment I'd abandoned. But I always knew our stay at her vacation home would be short-lived, so I only had to pack my hairbrush and a few dirty clothes I'd left lying at the foot of my guest bed. I'd plopped my bag on Fiona's bed and asked her to watch my stuff for me while I was gone.

Believe me, I didn't want to leave the family. They were going to consider me a flight risk until the day I died. But I would return for certain. I just had to let *someone* know so they didn't think I was kidnapped or dead or something.

"I know," I agreed with her. "I just need a head start. And I need you to make sure he doesn't come after me."

Fiona gathered her hair ties from the dresser and turned to me with a raised eyebrow. "Do you really think I can stop him?"

I sighed. "He's the one who claims this is so dangerous."

"It is!" Fiona hissed. "You should take all of us with you."

"Ryland doesn't even want me around, and you're all going after Matias anyway," I pointed out.

"Yes, because he's armed and highly dangerous." Fiona sat beside me on the bed. "He probably already has a witch lined up who's waiting on a big payday. Do you have any idea how dangerous it will be if he uses The Wise Owl? You wouldn't stand a chance against a vampire if you couldn't access your magic."

I frowned. "You've been talking to Venn, haven't you?"

"Well, yeah," Fiona admitted without shame.

"That's why you guys have to find Matias before he can use it," I said.

"Once we do, *then* we can go after Valkas. Together," she replied. "What's the rush, Rae? He's been hiding out for years. Why do you have to kill him *right now*?"

"There are a lot of reasons," I told her. I didn't think I could even begin to explain any of it. All I knew was I *had* to do it.

Maybe Synchrony was pushing me toward it or something… I mean, why would I get the dagger right now, right when the threat to lose my magic loomed over my head? I just had a gut feeling that Gregor Island was where I needed to be right now.

Fiona shifted on the bed. "I don't know, Rae. It doesn't feel right, none of it. It was too convenient that Matias just handed over the dagger he spent so long searching for. You could be a pawn."

I shrugged. "That's exactly what I am to him, and I'm okay with that. I'll deal with his successor once I kill Valkas."

Fiona nervously ran her fingers through her silky red hair. "I think you should talk to Sondra."

"No," I declined immediately. "You're the only person I trust to let me go."

Fiona bit her lower lip.

"Speaking of which," I said, glancing to the dark night sky. "It's time for me to leave. Maybe you can tell everyone I went to bed?"

Fiona's eyes glistened with tears. "You're so stubborn, Rae."

I smiled, glad someone understood me.

"You're like my long-lost sister," she said, wiping at her eyes. "I didn't want you to go so soon."

I leaned over and pulled her into a hug. "Do me a favor and kick Matias's ass for me?"

Fiona gave a nervous giggle and squeezed me back. "I'll get a good one in if I get a shot."

I drew away from her and swallowed down the lump in my throat. "I'll miss you."

Fiona's voice cracked. "I'll miss you, too."

I stood from the bed and crossed the room to the window, taking nothing with me but the clothes on my back.

"Rae?" Fiona called in a small voice before I shifted.

I turned back to her, and a knot formed in my chest. "Yeah?"

"Come back in one piece, okay?"

I hesitated before answering. I wasn't about to make a promise I couldn't keep. "I'll do my best."

Then I turned to the window, shifted, and flew off into the night.

2

____

I'd never flown over such a long distance before, but it was easy to follow the roads to Nocton. Once inside the city limits, Genevieve's house was simple to find.

I landed at the edge of her lawn and stared up at the dark bricks that matched the night sky. The windows were dark, like the rest of the houses on her street. For some reason, I pictured Genevieve as the kind of witch who would still be up at an ungodly hour, brewing potions in her cast iron cauldron. But even witches had to sleep. She'd make an exception for me, right?

I spent far too long staring at her house, contemplating my options. Did I go up and knock on the door, hoping she was still awake? Or did I wait until morning?

The sound of scuffling footsteps in the grass caught my attention a moment too late. I'd been wrapped up in my thoughts and let my guard down because I thought this was a safe street.

My head snapped in the direction of the noise just in time to see a tall, muscular figure diving for me. My heart lurched, and I spread my wings, but I wasn't fast enough. Hands clamped around my throat, slamming my raven body into the grass. Judging by how hard he squeezed, I had to guess he was human or witch. A vamp or shifter would have a much tighter hold on me—but that didn't change the fact that it still hurt.

I shifted immediately, hoping to startle the guy. It worked. He loosened his grip on me. I got my feet beneath him and dug them into his ribs, then kicked outward. He went flying across the lawn and landed with a *thud*. He gasped for breath but jumped to his feet quickly, taking on a defensive stance.

In the light from a nearby streetlamp, I was able to make out his features. He had light skin and dark hair that was just beginning to gray at the temples. There were age lines to his eyes that suggested he was in his late forties or early fifties. He had a straight nose and strong jaw, with a *successful busi-nessman* vibe going on. Except for the plaid pajama pants and white t-shirt.

"What the hell?" I snapped. Did this guy seriously think he could take on a shifter?

"I don't take kindly to shifters hanging around my house," he growled. "Who sent you?"

His house?

Before I could answer, the sound of the front door opening met my ears. I was relieved to see Genevieve poke her head outside. Her short hair was tame, and she wore a silky black nightgown.

"Are you going to stay out there all night?" she called across the space between us.

I glanced to Business Guy. The look he gave me said he didn't know whether she was talking to me or him.

"You'll have to forgive my husband," Genevieve said. "If I'd have known you were coming, I would've warned him."

Business Guy glared at me. "You two know each other?"

I straightened my shirt. "As a matter of fact, yes. And I don't appreciate being attacked for it."

His lips tightened. "You were acting suspicious."

"I was *standing* here!"

"Suspiciously," he muttered.

"That's enough," Genevieve snapped. "Richard, leave our poor guest alone. Rae, come inside. I don't have all night."

I hurried up the lawn to the front door. Genevieve didn't say anything as she pulled the door open to invite me inside. Richard followed, looking embarrassed.

"I'll see you when you're finished, darling." He took Genevieve's hand and kissed it before turning down the hall.

Only when he was out of sight did I finally speak. "I'm ready for that dagger," I said, glancing around, as if I expected someone to come bursting into the house looking for me.

"I figured you'd come for it soon." She gestured to the stairs for me to follow her.

"You're just going to hand it over?" I asked, shocked. "Just like that?"

"Yes," she said simply when we reached the top. "Your family asked me to keep it safe. They didn't say safe from whom."

I let out a snort. Totally embarrassing. Genevieve cocked an eyebrow at me.

"Clearly, you know I'm doing this without their blessing," I said.

Genevieve shrugged and led me into the room at the top of the stairs. "You don't need their blessing, do you? I, for one, would like to see you kill Valkas. Together, you and this dagger are his biggest weakness."

We entered a large room lined with dark bookshelves. The

drapes had been pulled over the two long windows at the other end of the room. Two plush black armchairs stood in front of a burning fire that cast shadows across the library.

Genevieve strolled over to the mantle, her nightgown billowing around her as she walked. "You'll have to excuse my husband," she said without looking back. "He's very protective and gets nervous about the kind of business I run. Please, take a seat."

I followed behind her and sank into one of the velvety chairs. My hands shook against the armrests. I couldn't believe I was going through with this. But at the same time, I never dreamed there was any other option.

Genevieve pulled a decorative box off the mantle and turned to me. It looked like a jewelry box and had a lock on the outside, though I didn't see a key anywhere in her hands. She sat across from me and waved her hand over the box. She muttered something under her breath that I couldn't under-stand, and the top popped open.

I inhaled a sharp breath when Genevieve turned the box toward me. The silver dagger sat on a bed of velvet material. I reached out, and my fingers curled around the handle of the blade. Warm tingles of magic spread up my arm. I felt powerful and unstoppable. *This mofo is going down!*

"Do you know how you're getting to the island?" Genevieve asked.

My grip tightened around the handle. "I was kind of going to wing it. I figured I could hitch a ride, then fly to the island."

Genevieve's eyebrows shot up. "You said it was in the middle of the Great Lakes, didn't you?"

I nodded.

"That's a long way to travel, considering you might miss it. I thought you said it was concealed by magic."

I shrugged. "I have pretty good endurance and a hell of a lot of determination. And it *was* concealed by magic—when Valkas was prisoner there."

Genevieve pressed her lips together. "If Valkas has even one witch on his side, it could very well still be concealed. The concealment charm won't be nearly as strong as the one that was on the island before he escaped, so it should be easy to break once you're close enough. The incantation *veritatem revelare*—reveal the truth—should work. The spell will be virtually undetectable since the island will only reveal itself to you and no one else. But the spell has a short range, so you have to know where you're going." She shot me a pointed expression, as if she didn't believe in me.

"I know where it is," I said confidently. I'd never forget where Clarita placed the mark on that map. It was my only connection to Jenna.

Genevieve stood. "Richard will drive you, then you'll take a boat as close as you can get to the island. You can fly the rest of the way. Remember the incantation."

"*Veritatem revelare,*" I repeated.

"Good," Genevieve said with a nod. "When would you like to leave?"

I hesitated. By now, Fiona had surely dropped the bomb on where I was headed. No doubt Venn was already on his way to stop me. What was his deal, anyway?

"As soon as possible," I answered.

"I'll have Richard get the car." Genevieve started toward the door, but she stopped halfway there and turned back toward me. "Oh, and Rae?"

"Yeah?" My throat tightened. I didn't like the tone of voice she used, as if she was about to break some terrible news.

Genevieve cleared her throat, but she held her head up

high and confident. "You should know that there's always more than one way off an island."

I furrowed my brow. It sounded ominous, like she thought I might get trapped on Gregor Island. "I thought witches couldn't tell the future."

She shook her head. "I can't. I'm just letting you know that even when strong bridges crumble, there's always another path to take."

3

I stood at the end of the marina, staring out into the vast water. It was like standing at the edge of the ocean. Water stretched across the landscape as far as the eye could see, and waves lapped at the rocky shore. Unlike the beautiful blue skies and clear water I'd seen when I visited the ocean as a kid, Lake Michigan was covered in a gray haze, and the horizon was invisible behind a dense layer of fog. The early morning air was cool, and I couldn't see the sun behind a thick layer of clouds. I wrapped my exposed arms around myself and clutched the dagger tightly in my hand.

Jenna was somewhere out there. I was so close to her now... yet so far away.

"Time to go."

I turned to see Richard standing behind me. He gestured to one of the motorboats parked at the edge of the dock and held tightly to the keys he'd rented.

"You know where you're going?" he asked with a raised eyebrow.

I nodded. "If you have a map, I can show you exactly where it is."

"Follow me."

I climbed onto the boat behind him. It was the nicest boat I'd ever been on, with an enclosed cabin and fancy leather seats for sunbathing. It wasn't big enough to live on, but I could probably sell it and buy a house in a cheap neighborhood.

Richard let me inside, and I pointed out our destination on the navigation screen. He started up the boat and began the long journey across the water. I stood outside the cabin, clutching on to the metal railing and letting the wind rush through my hair. I barely registered the cold air since I was concentrating so hard on the water in front of me, searching for any signs of a hidden island.

After what felt like hours, Richard slowed the boat until we left no wake behind.

"We're close," Richard said, "but we have a large area to search."

I closed my eyes, concentrating hard on the energy around me. If there was magic concealing the island, I should be able to feel it. I felt nothing but damp air on my skin.

"Keep going," I stated confidently.

Richard didn't even question me. He increased our speed slightly, though not as fast as before.

After several minutes, the faintest feeling of magic tingled across my arms like static electricity. I took another deep breath, letting out all the tension in my shoulders. My senses were on high alert. I heard the water lapping against the side of the boat, smelled and tasted the humidity in the air, and felt the faintest of breezes across my skin.

"We're getting closer," I said.

The farther we went, the more I felt that magical tingle. It was barely there, not nearly as powerful as the magic that radiated off The Wise Owl. I wouldn't have even felt it if I hadn't been paying attention. But it filled my heart with a sense of hope. Jenna didn't have to wait much longer.

Richard slowed the boat again as the fog thickened, blanketing the water until we could barely see in front of us.

"We're here," I said, more to myself than to Richard.

He pulled back on the throttle and killed the engine. The boat gently cut through the water, propelled along by our momentum. Without the sound of the engine to distract me, the magic felt stronger. It tingled up my arms and down my spine like a hundred tiny ants crawling across my skin.

"*The full moon is shining, the stars glitter above, the wind whispers softly, goodnight my love.*" I closed my eyes and whispered the tune to my mother's lullaby. I let it carry me to another place, a happy place, where all magic was possible.

In my head, her voice called back to me. *You can do this, Rachel.*

I was born to do this, I replied.

My eyes sprang open, and the incantation dropped from my lips. "*Veritatem revelare.*"

Straight in front of me, the fog parted, revealing huge boulders jutting out from the water fifty yards off the side of the boat. The boulders led like stepping stones to the edge of a rocky cliff. The cliff spanned hundreds of yards, but it barely covered the full length of the island. The island wasn't huge by any means, but it had to be at least fifty acres. Atop the cliff sat a lush green forest, full of all different types of trees, from deciduous varieties to evergreens. Just above the trees, I saw the peaks of a large building and several chimneys reaching up into the sky. It looked like it might be a mansion.

A sense of pride washed over me. I'd found it. I'd found Gregor Island!

I turned to Richard. "It's here."

His eyes continued to scan the water. He couldn't see it. The incantation Genevieve had given me only lifted the concealment charm for me.

"You're sure?" he asked.

"Yes. Please tell your wife thank you."

"Wait." Richard stopped me before I could leave. "Should I stay here and wait for you?"

I shook my head. I didn't know how long it would take me to find Jenna. "Your only job was to get me here. I'll find my own way back."

With that, I shifted and scooped up the dagger in my talons, then took off. I soared high above Gregor Island, trying to take in as much of the layout as I could. In the center of it all was a huge structure bigger than Maliya's mansion. It reminded me of a French chateau, with high towers stretching above the peaked roof. There were rows upon rows of windows set into the brick siding. A stone pathway led from the main doors and into the surrounding forest.

High above the island, I could see that the trees thinned into long, narrow strips that spiderwebbed away from the chateau. It looked like there were paths or roadways beneath me, but I couldn't see through the forest to the earth. One pathway led far away from the chateau, ending at a wide clearing that housed a cluster of small wood cabins. There must've been at least fifty of them. They reminded me of the single-room cabins we slept in at camp when I was a kid. There'd been enough room for two bunk beds and a small table in the corner to keep our stuff.

A sandy beach stretched out from the cabin community

and down to the shoreline. Two figures sat on the beach, but other than that, the community was quiet.

The cabins intrigued me. Why would the Soulless bother building cabins on their island if they already had a beautiful chateau to live in?

The answer struck me the moment I questioned it. The cabins were the blood slaves' quarters.

I dropped lower in the sky, swooping down to land on a tree branch near the farthest cabin from the beach. I clutched the dagger in one talon and the tree branch in the other, spreading my wings out to keep my body balanced until the limb stopped shaking beneath my weight. Curiously, I peered into one of the windows, but all I saw was darkness. I jumped to the next branch over, closer to the window. Still nothing. It looked as if a pair of dark curtains had been drawn closed, blocking my view of the inside.

If Jenna was here—and I knew she had to be—she'd no doubt be in one of these cabins. *Time to finally see my sister again.*

Flying over to the next tree branch, I came in closer to the second cabin and looked inside. I saw that the curtains were open and the window cracked. The daylight spilled inside just enough that I could see a figure lying on a bed, the sheets pulled up to his or her chin. I couldn't see the person's face, though, just the shape of a body sleeping there.

It could be Jenna, I thought hopefully.

Then the figure shifted. A mop of blond hair came into view, and I noticed the broad shoulders. Definitely not Jenna.

Inching my way down the branch and closer to the buildings, I peered into the third cabin's window. This one was arranged differently than the last. I could easily see two beds from my perch outside the window. Both were occupied, and each person's chest rose and fell slowly.

I glanced to the sky. The sun was hidden behind the clouds, but it must've been the middle of the day already. If everyone was asleep, it meant the Soulless had them on a schedule, one that kept them awake at night with the vampires.

The sound of breaking twigs stole my attention, and my gaze snapped in the direction of the noise. A man with skinny arms and a long nose tore through the forest. He wore a tattered white t-shirt with jeans and black boots, and a pair of keys jingled in his hands. He threw frightened glances behind his shoulder.

I went completely rigid, hoping he wouldn't spot me high above him in the tree. A huge black bird holding a dagger was more than a little suspicious.

To my relief, he didn't notice me. His feet skidded in the dirt as he nearly missed his turn. He caught himself and raced between the first two cabins. The sound of a door opening met my ears. I inched down my branch until I had a better view inside the second cabin. The blond mop-headed guy I'd seen sleeping sat bolt upright in bed, frightened by the arrival of his roommate.

"What the bloody hell?" Mop Head snapped before lowering his voice, which carried through the open window. "What are you doing?"

"I'm done with this shit," Skinny Guy breathed. "It's time to go."

"What?" Mop Head replied in disbelief.

"I said *it's time to go*," Skinny Guy emphasized. "We're getting off this island." He dangled the keys in front of Mop Head's face, grinning.

Mop Head's eyes widened in horror. "Are you insane?"

Skinny Guy shrugged. "Maybe a little."

"Did you just steal the keys to the Soulless' boat?" Mop Head hissed. "Do you have any idea—?"

I didn't hear the rest of what he said as the sound of an engine roared through the forest. Not just one engine, I quickly realized. An entire fleet of them. And they were coming right this way.

I shrank further back into the trees to conceal myself, but I kept my eyes on the cabin window. Mop Head was out of bed now, his fists clenched tightly as he hissed in low whispers at his roommate. I couldn't hear what he was saying, but it did *not* look good. Skinny Guy tried to make a run for it, but Mop Head grabbed him by the collar.

"I'm *not* taking the fall for this!" he shouted.

Just then, an ATV came tearing through the forest at high-speed. It was just a blur on the other side of the cabins. The four-wheeler stopped abruptly in front of Skinny Guy's cabin. He'd left the door open, so I could see some of what was going on. At least six other ATVs stopped behind it.

Skinny Guy and Mop Head were engaged in a scuffle now, fighting for the keys that had fallen on the floor. Mop Head was telling him to give the keys back, while Skinny Guy was shouting for them to make a run for it.

"Do you know what you've done?" Mop Head demanded. "You've killed us both!"

I stared through the window and out the open door, my eyes locked on the large figure riding the first ATV. Every inch of his body was covered in black clothing. He even wore a long-sleeved turtleneck shirt, with leather gloves and a tinted black motorcycle helmet.

He swung his leg over the seat of his four-wheeler and

stood, throwing his shoulders back confidently. He must've been at least six-foot-five, with broad shoulders and thick biceps. His footsteps were heavy, *thudding* against the earth as if in warning.

Skinny Guy and Mop Head both went silent. Their bodies trembled as they turned to look at him.

It wasn't until the guy stepped inside the cabin that he pulled his helmet off. He was hauntingly beautiful, with a straight nose, strong jaw, and piercing silver eyes. He had pale skin and dirty blond hair. Most girls would swoon over him. Me? I was already itching to drive my dagger through his heart.

Rage knitted in his tight eyebrows, and his jaw clenched. The man looked terrifying when he was angry, like he could snap a person in half in one swift, strong motion. Though he was conventionally attractive, there was *nothing* beautiful about him. It was like he brought a darkness with him when he stepped into the room. And I knew exactly why.

The man was Valkas.

I'd seen photos of him before. They always gave me an uneasy feeling, and my guts twisted at the sight of him. Seeing him up close was even worse. After everything he'd done, I prayed he would suffer a fate far worse than my dagger.

Valkas smirked. He didn't even glance at the men as he pulled the leather gloves off his hands, finger by finger. "Well, well, well… what do we have here?" There was a hint of a British accent to his tone, but it was muddled, like he'd been to enough areas of the world that no single accent had stuck with him.

Skinny Guy dropped the keys at Valkas's feet and backed up slowly. "We… we found these in the woods."

Valkas finally looked up, then cocked his head. "Is that so?"

The words rolled off his tongue like poison. "Because my men say someone with your description stole them from the boathouse."

Mop Head dropped to his knees. "Please, sir. Spare me. I had no idea."

Valkas's arm swung out, and the back of his hand cracked against the side of Mop Head's face. I flinched, but I couldn't tear my eyes away.

"You'll speak only when spoken to!" Valkas roared. His face twisted in rage, and spittle flew from his mouth. "And I will be addressed as *Lord* for as long as you live on this godforsaken island."

Lord Valkas. Oh God. This guy was worse than I thought. And vain as hell.

I should've gone in there and killed him on the spot, but there were five other faceless guys standing behind him, their arms crossed. They all wore motorcycle helmets, so I couldn't see their eyes, but I guessed they were all vamps. There was only one man, a sixth one, whose skin was exposed. He was almost as big as Valkas, with tan skin and slicked-back dark hair. I was strong, but not strong enough to fight them all off at once. I had to attack Valkas when he was alone. And until then, I couldn't risk exposing myself... no matter what.

"*You*," Valkas snarled, turning on Skinny Guy.

"I-I'm sorry, sir—Lord," Skinny Guy stuttered, lowering his head. "It won't happen again, Lord Valkas."

Valkas smirked. "No, I don't imagine it will."

In the blink of an eye, Valkas's hand shot forward, slamming Skinny Guy into the wall as his hand sank into his chest. Skinny Guy's eyes went as wide as golf balls, and his mouth hung open, as if he was trying to inhale a breath that didn't come. My whole body gave a start. I thought my eyes were playing tricks on me, until Valkas pulled away, producing a deep red meaty organ the size of his fist. *A heart.*

It was like watching a scene from a horror movie, except it was playing out right in front of my eyes. I was beyond nauseous. Normally, I could handle this kind of thing, but my head spun, and I had to grip on tighter to the tree branch to keep from falling to the ground. The sick sensation that slammed into my gut only lasted a split second before rage bubbled up to replace it. Valkas was pure evil, and he was going straight to hell if I had anything to say about it.

Skinny Guy's limp body slumped down the wall and to the floor. Mop Head kept his head low and didn't make a sound, no doubt afraid that he'd be next.

Valkas didn't even spare him a glance as he strolled out the door, the warm, fresh heart still clutched in his hands. He didn't even bother placing the helmet back on his head to protect his skin from the sun. There was a thick enough cloud cover that I was sure he'd only walk away with mere first-degree burns.

"I know you're all awake!" Valkas boomed. "All slaves are to be out of their cabins by the time I count to five. One… Two… Three…"

All throughout the community, cabin doors began to swing open. People flooded out onto the dirt paths. I couldn't see most of them, but I could hear the scuffle of footsteps. Valkas paced along the dirt path and out of my view.

I hesitated. I didn't come all this way just to be caught. But the temptation was just too great. I *had* to see if Jenna was somewhere in that mass of people.

I spread my wings and lifted off my perch, landing on the roof of the cabin. I clutched the dagger tightly in one talon and hopped forward until I could see Valkas below me.

He held the heart high above his head for everyone to see. "Four... Five."

Men and women stood outside their cabins in their pajamas. I expected them to be clutching each other and crying in fear, but all emotion was hidden away. It was like they'd come to expect this level of violence from Valkas, like they knew they'd be punished for cowering in fear of him. One woman slid her hand into another lady's fingers, and a male had paled to the point where he looked like he might vomit. Other than that, the blood slaves swallowed down their disgust.

My eyes scanned the crowd, and my heart *pitter-pattered* in anticipation. I didn't see Jenna anywhere.

"*This* is what happens to people who steal from me," Valkas boomed. "See to it that it doesn't happen again."

Valkas flung the heart across the ground, snarling in disgust. He turned away before it finished rolling. It stopped at a woman's feet, coated in dirt. She took a step back, unable to hide the horror in her expression.

Valkas didn't even notice. He licked the blood from his fingers and turned to the guy with the slicked-back hair. He gestured to the cabin. "Clean this mess up, Rogers."

Stoically, he placed his gloves back on his hands, like the remaining blood didn't bother him one bit. One of his men hurried over with Valkas's helmet. Valkas snatched it from his hands and situated it on his head as he swung his leg over the seat of the ATV. The engine roared to life, and he sped off into the forest. Three of his men took off behind him, while the other three stayed to follow orders.

Everyone remained frozen like statues as Rogers stepped forward. He waved his hand, and the next thing I knew, Skinny Guy's body was floating out of the cabin like it was suspended by invisible ropes.

A witch, I realized in disgust. What kind of person would pledge himself to the Soulless? Valkas must've promised a very generous deal.

The witch dropped the body, slumping it over the back of one of the ATVs. My stomach twisted at the sight of Skinny Guy's eyes staring lifelessly toward the sky.

It wasn't until Valkas's men had disappeared into the woods behind him that the people below me finally moved. They all took a collective breath, as if they'd been holding it until now. Even I hadn't realized my lungs were about to implode from the pressure. I inhaled deeply through my beak, trying to shake off the uneasy feeling that had settled in my feathers.

For the first time since Valkas's arrival, emotions began to cross people's faces. The whole clearing broke out into whispers. People grabbed on to each other for comfort. One girl threw her hand over her mouth and raced behind a cabin to spew her guts. Another dropped to her knees and covered her face with her hands while she cried. Two guys came up behind her and settled gentle, comforting hands on her shoulders.

"We're here for you," one of them told her.

Three other women quickly joined them, surrounding the younger woman to make sure she was all right. At least six people entered the cabin I was perched on top of. I could hear their voices reassuring Mop Head.

"It's not your fault," a male voice said.

"We'll get this cleaned up," a woman added.

It struck me how much these people cared for each other. No one turned into their cabins to leave the mess for someone else. They acted like one big family, like a community.

It should've warmed my heart, but I was still shaking in rage. Valkas had aptly named his gang of vampires. *Soulless.* How could anyone with a soul be capable of such evil?

The young woman couldn't stop her sobs. The group surrounding her helped her to her feet and into a nearby cabin. My breathing grew ragged as the sound of her cries echoed in my ears.

This is what happens to people who steal from me.

Surely theft wasn't worthy of a death sentence. The man was an innocent captive; of course he wanted a way off this island. I didn't even want to think about what the Soulless had done to him to drive him toward risking his life like that.

Whatever it was, I couldn't sit around contemplating the possibilities. My gaze swept across the clearing again, but Jenna was nowhere in sight. Every fiber of my being told me that Jenna was somewhere on this island. If she wasn't here with the other blood slaves, that meant she must've been up at the chateau. I'd go there, find Jenna, and kill Valkas. Once he and his men were gone, I'd get all these people safely off Gregor Island.

Mind made up, I launched myself into the air in the direction of the chateau.

4

I swooped down at a back entrance to the building. The trees were close and concealed me, but since I didn't see anyone nearby, I shifted into human form. It'd be easier to navigate around the chateau that way. Glancing upward toward the tall windows, I saw that the curtains were drawn on all of them. After determining the coast was clear, I raced across the space between the trees and the backdoor, keeping the dagger clutched tightly in my hand.

The doorknob twisted easily, and I peeked inside. I breathed a sigh of relief when I saw that the hallway was empty. Quietly, I slipped in. I was careful to close the door behind me as softly as I could. As a shifter, the vampires wouldn't hear me coming by my heartbeat or my breathing, but they'd definitely hear a door banging shut and announcing my arrival.

I started down the narrow hallway, taking soft steps. Light flickered across the walls from the fire within the sconces on the walls. It definitely gave off a *haunted house* vibe, which only made me smile. Haunted houses were totally my thing.

The various doorways on either side of the hall were all closed, so I couldn't see where they led. I itched to peek into one of the doors just to see if Jenna was inside, but I wasn't too keen on waking a group of vampires. I'd scope everything out first to get a feel for where Jenna might be.

I reached the end of the hall and came to a second hallway. This one was wider than the last, with big arches cut out in the wall that revealed a huge seating area. The drapes were drawn, and a huge candelabra chandelier hung from the ceiling, lighting up the room. There were no lamps or overhead bulbs, no electricity of any kind, and that gave the place an even more unique, antique vibe.

I could hardly take in the grandeur of the chateau. Whoever had designed it certainly had good taste. The floors were all polished hardwood and the walls were plain white, but there was an architectural beauty to the place. In the large room beyond the arches, sofa upon sofa sat elegantly arranged in various seating areas, with a big grand piano in the corner. Had this really been where Valkas had been imprisoned all those years? I'd been picturing him hanging out in a deep, dark cave or something on a deserted island. This place was practically a castle.

A door banged loudly toward the end of the wide hallway, where I could see it opened up to a large foyer. I caught sight of a group of men in dark clothing and immediately crouched down low. Peeking around the corner, I saw Valkas's three men remove their helmets. As I predicted, they all had matching pale skin.

"Caleb, wake the girls and bring them to my room." Valkas's voice carried down the hall. "Punishing slaves makes me thirsty."

The girls? Blood slaves?

Jenna!

I shot up from where I was crouched but hesitated. My eyes followed the men as they dispersed. Valkas started up a grand staircase, while the other men went in opposite directions. I had no way of knowing which one was Caleb. Otherwise, I would've followed the bastard to find my sister.

There was only one other easy solution. Follow Valkas and wait for Caleb to bring Jenna back to his room.

One of the vamps was headed my way, so I crept back down the hall and crouched behind a long, decorative table. I held my breath as the vamp continued past the large sitting room with the grand piano in it.

As soon as I heard his footsteps fade, I was back on my feet, peeking out into the wider hallway. It was deserted, so I took my chance and hurried down it. My heart slammed against my rib cage, but not because I was scared. If anything, I was *excited*. I was going to see my sister again. These vampires were going to die at my hand. This was a freaking thrill ride!

When I reached the foyer, the sound of footsteps in the hall above the grand staircase met my ears. I glanced around quickly, but the foyer was empty. The only decorations were mirrors and paintings on the walls, unlike the rest of the chateau, where there was a sofa, table, dresser, or some other piece of furniture every few feet. I rushed into the corner beneath the stairs and held my breath, praying that whomever it was wouldn't see me through the darkness.

Who was I kidding? It was sure to be a vampire. If he took one look at where I stood, he wouldn't miss me. I held my dagger up, poised for attack if it came to that.

The man's footsteps pounded down the stairs above my

head. When he reached the bottom, he slipped his motorcycle helmet back on and exited out the front doors.

I remained frozen in the corner, forcing my breathing to slow and listening to the sounds around me. The building was eerily quiet. Taking my chance, I rushed out of the shadows and hurried up the stairs with light footsteps.

When I reached the top, I found a maze of hallways, all veering off in different directions. I had no way of knowing which way I'd find Valkas. So I took a wild guess. I started down the hallway to my left, passing by door after door. Something told me Valkas's room would be a bit over the top and easy to spot, so I skipped all the plain doors and headed to the pair of double doors at the end of the hall. I pressed my ear to it and heard muffled voices inside.

"Lord Valkas does not like to be woken in the middle of the day," a gruff voice said.

Definitely not Valkas's. The way he spoke, it didn't even sound like Valkas was in the room, but I continued listening to be sure.

"This incident will reflect poorly on all of us," Gruff Voice continued.

"Yes, of course, sir," another man replied.

"This never should've happened in the first place," Gruff Voice said. "If you men down at the boathouse were paying the slightest bit of attention, it wouldn't have." He spoke in such a harsh tone that it made me flinch. "See to it that it doesn't happen again."

"Yes, sir. It won't."

"Excuse me a moment," Gruff Voice interrupted.

Silence followed for several seconds. I had no idea what was going on behind that door. Then the sound of the floor creaking just on the other side met my ear.

I leapt away instantly and took the first hiding place I could find—a large, decorative vase situated in the corner of the hall. I shrank to my raven form and hugged the wall, holding my breath. My dagger had fallen from my hand and lay at my feet.

I heard the door swing open. In the reflection from one of the mirrors on the wall, I saw a man stick his head out the door and glance around. Something in his features hinted at old age, but his skin had been smoothed out, and there wasn't a gray hair on his head. Freaking vampire curse turning them all into the most beautiful versions of themselves. It was like cosmetics on steroids.

He narrowed his silver eyes and pursed his lips, looking so angry it rivaled Valkas's terrifying features. The man gave me chills.

He stood there for what felt like a full minute, frozen in the doorway. If it weren't for his eyes scanning the hall, I might've mistaken him for a statue. He sniffed the air.

He can't smell me, I told myself as reassurance. It was true that he couldn't smell me the way he could smell humans, but perhaps he could sense me in other ways? The metallic smell of my dagger? The scent of laundry detergent on my clothes? Perhaps he could even sense the shift in the air when I breathed.

Usually by now I would've already staked the vamp through the heart, not giving him enough time to assess my presence, but I wasn't about to alert the whole house I was here. Killing him would be reckless and stupid and... *fun.*

He stepped out into the hall. I could see his polished black shoe from where I crouched behind the vase.

He doesn't see you. He'll give up, I told myself.

But I was a liar. Because he'd already seen me, and his hand was headed straight for me.

Instinct took over. I shifted just before his fingers touched my feathers. In a quick motion, I threw my hands upward to connect with his wrist as I ducked out of the way. I used my strength against his agility, following the momentum of his hand upward. And then I yanked down, causing him to flip through the air and land with a hard *thud* on the floor.

I reached for my dagger. Before I had my fingers around the handle, he'd already leapt to his feet. His knee swung upward, connecting with my nose. Pain shot out through my face, which turned out to be a blessing. He caught sight of the blood trickling down my face and paused momentarily. Hunger burned in his eyes.

It was just enough time for me to kick my leg out beneath him and knock him back on his ass. Before he could react, I was on top of him, shoving my dagger through his heart. He crumbled into a pile of ash beneath me.

I didn't even have a moment to relish in my victory. A split second later, the second guy was in the doorway. This man was younger than the last, though he had the same good looks. A moment of shock crossed his silver eyes.

I leapt to my feet and sprang on him. He reeled backward and slammed into one of the bookshelves in the room. He spread his arms out to catch himself. His fingers curled around one of the thick books, and he hurled it at me. The thick, pointed corner smashed just above my right eyebrow, making me see red.

I cursed under my breath, clutching my forehead, which was warm and sticky from blood. All he did was smirk.

"That freaking hurt, jackhole," I snapped at him.

"I've got plenty more where that came from." He wiggled

his eyebrows and lifted another book. "Who are you, and what are you doing here?"

"Seriously?" I asked, totally unamused. "We're going to talk this out?"

He hurled the second book at me, but I ducked. It soared over my head and crashed into a shelf on the other side of the room.

I sprang back to my feet. "Hey, now. We don't want to wake everyone."

"Then tell me who you are," he demanded.

"So you can kill me?" I shrugged. "Nah, I'm not really one for talking."

He cracked his knuckles. "Have it your way."

He dove toward me. His shoulder smashed into my abdomen, and his arms curled around my middle. I didn't even try to dodge out of the way. I let him take me to the ground.

As his fingers clamped around my throat, I swung my dagger downward into his back. His eyes went wide, and he inhaled a sharp breath, then... nothing. His clothes fell on top of me as his body turned to ash.

I squeezed my eyes shut and closed my mouth to keep from getting it in my face. I felt the ash rain down on my skin, but I shook it off.

After I sat up, I used the guy's suit to wipe the blood from my face. Outside the door, I grabbed Gruff Voice's clothes, cleaned up as much ash from both of them as I could, and shoved their clothes into a drawer in the desk across the room. Surely, I didn't have long before someone noticed the two were missing, but I didn't need someone walking in on the evidence and launching a search party before I got Jenna out of here.

Once completed, I hurried out of the library and down the hall. When I reached the top of the balcony where I'd started, I decided to try the hall to the right. It was identical to the last, only mirrored. I got the strangest sense of *déjà vu*.

When I reached the pair of double doors on the end, they were open a crack. I tiptoed forward and peeked inside.

At first, I saw nothing but an empty four-poster bed. Thin red fabric draped across the canopy, and the sheets were crumpled up in the middle, as if the owner had just gotten out of bed.

Then I saw him. The blond hair, the broad shoulders… it was definitely Valkas. I couldn't take my eyes off of him as he paced around the room. He looked distressed as he raked his fingers through his hair, then curled his hands into fists at his sides. Just looking at him made my insides burn with rage. All I could think about were all the people he'd killed when he'd rampaged across the States eight years ago. All the people he'd changed into vampires and the ones that they'd killed and enslaved in turn. How he'd forced Elizabeth to cast the spell that changed him. He was a monster then, and he was a monster now.

But worse than all of that, he'd ordered his men to kidnap my sister. And I'd be damned if he didn't pay for that.

He was alone. No one was around. All that stood between me and him was a thin wooden door. All it took was one move, one stab through the heart.

Now was my time, before Caleb returned with the girls. I could hardly believe this was happening. All I had to do was slip inside and kill him. This would all be over soon.

Valkas sat on the bed with his back to the door. He reached for an unlit candle on the nightstand and tilted it to the one that was burning.

Now! Do it now!

I didn't second guess the little voice in my head. I pushed on the door, and it swung easily under my weight just enough for me to slip inside. I felt like a ninja as I tiptoed across the floor. My footsteps were so quiet across the carpet that Valkas didn't notice me. He was too preoccupied lighting his candles.

My heart pummeled against my rib cage as I lifted my dagger, careful not to make a noise. I held my breath so tightly it felt like my lungs might explode. But I barely noticed, because I was on Valkas's island, in his chateau, in his bedroom, and I was half a second away from killing him.

The world would rejoice. I didn't even care if anyone recognized me for what I'd done. All I cared about was getting rid of the vampires once and for all.

Goodbye, filthy vamps! No one will miss you.

I thrust my blade downward.

But my hand never made it to his back. Valkas whirled around and caught my wrist without half an inch to spare. My heart leapt into my throat. He yanked on me so hard it felt like my arm was going to rip off, spun me around, and pinned me to the bed.

Holy hell! Vamps were fast, but I'd never seen one move *that* fast! I probably had freaking whiplash from the bastard.

"Mm…" He straddled me, pressing my hips into the bed and leaning in so closely that I could smell the copper on his breath. "What's this?"

Hell! What have I done?

My mind instantly flickered to Venn. Maybe he'd been right.

Valkas's eyes roamed over me, and he inhaled deeply. Pleasure crossed his expression, and I thought I might throw up in his face. I tried to struggle out of his hold, but the vamp was holding on tight. He was even stronger than Ryland. He squeezed my wrist so tightly I knew it would bruise, but I didn't drop the dagger. I only curled my fingers around it tighter.

"A shifter?" he asked with a smirk, biting his lower lip like it pleased him. "And not one of mine."

"I'm not here to talk," I snapped, then I threw my head forward into his nose.

The top of my head throbbed from where they'd connected, but he barely reacted apart from tightening his hold on me. I writhed beneath him, trying to find a way free. But I'd already broken my one rule about vampires. *Never let them get the upper hand.*

Valkas laughed, a terrible laugh that made me nauseous. "Oh, you're a fighter, too?" he mocked.

"Go to hell." I spit in his face.

He didn't even bother wiping it from his eyes. Instead, he leaned down until his lips were at my ear. For a second, I thought he might bite me, which by the way was a total *never gonna happen.*

But he didn't bite me. All he did was whisper in my ear. And those words were enough to make my blood run cold.

"I'm going to have fun with you."

5

I thrust my hips upward. It bought me just enough space to turn to the side. I grabbed hold of one of the bed posts with my free hand and yanked myself across the bed. I managed to get one foot free, and I kicked it up under his chin.

He responded by tugging hard on my arm, throwing me back down on the bed. I held in my cry of pain as the muscles in my shoulder tore. I kicked my feet out again, trying to struggle free, but he knelt on top of my chest, looming over me. He pressed down so hard that I gasped for breath.

"*Ardeat ignis,*" I muttered under my breath. I expected fire to come shooting out of my palms and burn his hand, but all that happened was the surface of my skin heated a little.

"*Fulgur.*" I tested the incantation for lightning. Nothing happened.

Reality hit me like a ton of bricks. My magic wasn't going to save me this time.

Valkas laughed. "A shifter *and* a witch? Such a wonderful

combination." Squeezing my wrists tightly with one hand, he wrenched the dagger from me with the other.

It was my one hope of making it out of here alive. If I couldn't fight him when he was alone and unarmed with the one weapon in the world that could kill him, how did I ever stand a chance? I felt all my hope drain out of me at once, and I began to panic. I clawed at anything I could: his face, his arms, and the leg pressing down on my chest. Every inch of my body felt alive with fire as a panicked rage tore through me. I would've screamed if I could catch my breath.

"Now, now, dear shifter," he said calmly, eyeing the dagger with interest. "If you don't start treating me with respect, I may just have to use your very own weapon on you."

Like hell you will!

I threw my fist so hard at his face that his body lifted off of me. I inhaled a greedy breath the same time my foot swung outward and connected with his hand. The dagger flew out of his grasp and slid across the floor toward the door. I immediately jumped off the bed and dove for it.

Mid-air, something caught my foot, and I fell to the ground with a hard crash. I caught myself, but I was a half an inch away from a second bloody nose. A split-second later, I felt my body being dragged across the floor, away from the dagger. I reached out for anything, clawing at the carpet. My hand finally found the foot of the bed, and I grabbed on tight.

To my surprise, Valkas dropped me. I sprang to my feet again, but he was in front of me in less than a second, blocking my path to the dagger and to the door.

I wasn't about to give up so easily. After a split-second to come up with a plan, I swung out my leg and my heel connected with one of the bed posts. The entire thing shattered, sending wood splinters everywhere. The top beam of the canopy sagged without its support. I grabbed the closest splinter—a big, thick one with a sharp, jagged end—and held it out in front of me.

Valkas stood still but looked ready for me, like I was some little puppy he was trying to corner. "Oh, darling," he sang. "It'd be a shame to kill you. You amuse me. That isn't going to kill me."

"It will certainly slow you down," I replied.

Valkas's lips curled up into an evil smirk. "You are quite the resolute assassin, aren't you?"

"*Resolute assassin?*" I repeated, narrowing my eyes at him.

Valkas waved his hand. "Yes, *resolute*. Determined. Unwavering. You'll do whatever it takes to fulfill your cause."

"I know what it means," I snapped. "And you're damn straight I'll do whatever it takes."

I lunged for him again. I swore I almost had him, but he dodged at the last millisecond and used my momentum against me. His palm slammed into my back, sending me smashing into the floor so hard it knocked the wind out of me.

Valkas reached for the red sheet on the bed and tore a chunk off so fast I barely saw it. He jumped on top of me again and pinned my wrists together. He tried to tie the fabric around them, but it only tore as I fought against it. I smirked a little. Even Lord Valkas couldn't keep this girl tied down.

The sound of footsteps in the hall caught my ears. Was that a glimmer of hope I heard?

"Out!" Valkas shouted before I could even turn to see who it was.

I heard the door click shut. *Well, crap!*

"You want to play rough?" Valkas growled in my ear. "We'll play rough."

His hand fisted in my hair, and he tugged *hard*.

"Ow!" I cried, cursing.

His palm cracked against the side of my face so hard my head spun. Then I felt the cool metal of the dagger touch my neck. I immediately went still. Valkas's face swam in front of my view.

"Why are you here?" he demanded.

"You killed my parents. Kidnapped my sister. Murdered thousands. Take your pick," I replied, disgusted.

Valkas smiled, like I wasn't listing off his crimes but rather his accomplishments. "I'll take them all, darling."

Ew! Was he going to keep calling me that? It sounded horrible on his tongue.

"Or you could just go to hell," I retorted.

The dagger pressed tighter against my skin. This was it. I was going to die. Somehow, I kind of always knew it'd happen at the hands of a vampire, though I'd always hoped it wouldn't. At least it would be quick. Better to die at the hands of a vampire than to be turned into one.

But he didn't. He just sat there looming over me, his nostrils flaring.

"Go on. Do it," I insisted. "Why aren't you killing me?"

He tilted his head. "And risk you reincarnating just to come after me again? I don't think so."

The blood drained from my face, and my breathing stalled. How did he know?

Valkas drew away from me slowly. It was almost like he was letting me go, but I couldn't just leave now. He stood and sat on the bed, leaving me on the floor. I pushed myself to a sitting position, but I otherwise didn't move. For one, I was dead if I did. And two, I had questions that needed answering.

"Funny thing about this dagger," Valkas said, like he was sitting down a child to tell them a story. "I've seen it before. It's the only thing that can kill me." His eyes darted from the dagger to me, and he stared at me with those evil eyes. "*But,* there's only one person in the world who can use it. Another has tried and didn't succeed. What makes you think you can?"

My jaw tensed, and I kept it locked tight. The way he asked the question suggested he already knew the answer.

Valkas stood and began pacing around the room. My heart pummeled against my rib cage. I was starting to question that whole haunted house thing. It wasn't as fun when the real monsters came out to play.

"I have a theory," Valkas announced. "I think that bastard who staked this dagger through my heart eight years ago realized his mistake. I think he went searching for the one person who could kill me." His eyes connected with mine. "And I think he found her."

Oh, shit! Nothing gets past this guy, does it?

I swallowed hard. "And what if he did?"

He leaned against the desk in the corner, looking amused. "Then I think I'm going to trap her soul. But first, I'm going to have some fun with her."

I clenched my jaw. "And what if she, say, kills herself before you could do that? Assuming you even *know* how to trap a soul."

Valkas smirked. "I have my ways. But I trust that she'll keep herself alive. Because if she doesn't do *exactly* as I say, I'll torture her sister to the point where it'll make the devil look like a fairytale hero."

My knees shook, and they weren't even holding me up. "You're bluffing," I accused. "I want to see her."

Valkas straightened. "Oh, darling. I *never* bluff when it comes to torture. I'll let Jenna know you said hello."

Time altogether stopped when he said my sister's name. What. The. Hell?

Valkas grinned and spread his arms out wide. "Shall we begin?"

6

I had to remind myself that there were certain things in life far worse than death. Death wasn't actually that scary once I thought about it. I'd certainly miss Jenna if she died, the same way I missed my parents, but at least she'd be free of captivity. At least she'd have a chance to reincarnate and start over again.

But if I didn't comply, Valkas would torture her. I couldn't even bring myself to think about the things he would do to her, considering he was the guy who just this morning had ripped a guy's heart fresh from his chest. What would Jenna endure if I didn't do as I was told?

My body shuddered just thinking about it.

"I want to see proof she's still alive," I demanded.

Valkas clicked his tongue. "I don't negotiate."

I didn't trust Valkas one bit, but I found myself trusting him on this. Jenna was here, and he *would* torture her to hurt me.

I wasn't the kind of girl who did as she was told. I went against all the rules if I thought it was the right thing to do.

But right now, complying was the right thing. It was the only way to spare Jenna from Valkas's wrath.

But dammit, it was hard.

"On your knees," Valkas demanded.

I went rigid for a moment. My body didn't want to comply, even though my mind did.

Valkas stepped forward threateningly. "I'm not going to ask you again. On. Your. Knees."

I swallowed down the lump rising in my throat and pushed myself to my knees.

Valkas gave a triumphant smirk. It was clear his power over me brought him pleasure. It made me sick.

"Very good," he said as he paced around me. "Now shift."

I didn't. Not right away. I had to let him know that I wasn't going to be some mindless follower. I would fight. Not now, but once Jenna was safe, I would.

I held out just long enough for him to inhale another breath. Then I did as I was told.

As soon as my body shrank to my raven form, Valkas reached down and grabbed me. His fingers tightened under my wings, forcing them outward. He lifted me and looked me in the eye. I responded with a calm expression, mostly just to piss him off.

"Hold still, darling," Valkas whispered. "This will only hurt a little."

Before I knew what was happening, he tossed me onto the bed and pinned me to the mattress. I gasped for breath as my face pressed into the sheets. I pumped my wings in protest.

Valkas tugged *hard* at the end of my right wing, then pain shot up through it. Shortly after, the pain radiated up my left. It was a sharp, tender pain, as if he'd just ripped my fingernails from the nail beds.

Suddenly, Valkas's weight lifted off of me. I inhaled a deep breath and squawked. I flapped my wings on instinct to distance myself from him. I managed to kick myself to the edge of the bed, but I stumbled off of it and crashed to the floor.

What the hell? Why couldn't I fly? What had Valkas done to me? The calm, collected façade I'd put on only moments ago completely vanished.

"You can shift back now," Valkas offered.

I finally looked at him, and what I saw caused my stomach to bottom out. Valkas paced to the other side of the room with a large handful of black feathers clutched in his hands.

Mine!

I glanced to my wings to see that my flight feathers had been ripped out, making my wings look shorter and disproportionate. He'd done it so I couldn't escape the island! Evil didn't even begin to cover it. I'd never felt so violated in my life. Every fiber of my being told me to attack, to fight, but the little voice in the back of my head reminded me of Jenna.

So I didn't move. I lay there on the floor, letting the pain pulse through my wings and thinking about all the horrible things I'd do to Valkas when given the chance.

If given the chance, I corrected myself. I'd had my chance, and I'd screwed it up. Valkas wasn't like the normal vampires I fought. He was faster and stronger, not to mention he had an army of vampires *and* a witch to do his bidding for him.

"On second thought, stay in your shifted form." Valkas's voice cut through the silence. "I think you'll be more comfortable that way." The way he said it didn't sound the least bit comforting.

The pain in my wings disappeared as a numbness took

over. *Hopeless.* That was the one word that went through my head. How had I strolled in here with so much determination and confidence only to end up here, a prisoner to the Soulless?

After dropping the dagger and my feathers on a desk opposite the bed, Valkas picked up a small metal object I didn't get a good look at.

He approached me again. I didn't protest as he reached down and lifted me by the neck. He held me away from him as if I was a piece of dirty garbage.

I just hung there, a million thoughts racing through my mind all at once. This couldn't be it, could it? There had to be a way out of here. A way to get that dagger back. A way to find Jenna. A way to get off this island.

Valkas left the room and turned down a hall I hadn't been down. The first thing I noticed was a thick black wire cage sitting upon a table at the end of the hall, surrounded by fake red rose blossoms. Dim light from the few wall sconces reflected off a mirror hanging above the table.

All throughout the chateau there were decorative arrangements placed on narrow tables, hung on the walls, or situated in the corners. At first glance, the bird cage looked like a beautiful decoration, until I realized his intention. This decoration just so happened to serve Valkas's purpose perfectly. My whole body tensed as Valkas opened the cage and shoved me inside. The cage was small and cramped. If I tried to shift, it'd squash me.

Valkas opened his hand to reveal the metal object he'd brought with him. A padlock. He placed the lock around the wire bars and shot me a devilish grin. "Sweet dreams."

Then he turned on his heel and retreated down the hall.

I sat there with a clenched beak, watching him go. He

could enjoy my captivity all he wanted. I'd play his game for now, but one way or another, I was getting out of here.

"Rachel." Venn wrapped me in his arms, pulling me close to him. The scent of home filled my nose, and my whole body warmed under his touch. I saw nothing as I buried my face into his shoulder.

"Venn, I'm so sorry. I should've listened to you."

"I missed you," he whispered, pressing his nose in my hair. "You have no idea how worried I was."

I drew away from him to look him in the eyes. His eyes were warm and welcoming. I became so lost in them that I didn't even register our surroundings. We could've been floating through space for all I knew.

"But I had to do it," I told him. "I had to at least try."

"But you failed," Venn argued.

"No." I shook my head, refusing to believe it. "This isn't over yet."

"It's fine." Venn pulled me back into a tight hug, and I relaxed into his embrace. "All that matters is that you're safe with me now."

"But I'm not, Venn," I stated. "Not yet."

The sound of a door slamming startled me awake. I hadn't even realized I'd drifted off. I squawked and spread my wings, but the tender ends hit the edges of the cage, sending a fresh wave of pain through my wings. The memory of my dream resurfaced, and my heart ached for Venn. I hadn't been gone long, but I already missed him. I wished he'd come with me.

A man walking through the hall turned to glance at me. He had pale skin and silver eyes. No surprise there. He looked confused by my presence but continued on down the hall. A few moments later, another door opened and a woman emerged from the room. She had the same silver eyes, but dark hair and young features.

"Hey, Kyle!" she called, catching up with the other vamp. She moved down the hallway quicker than any human and stuck her arm in the crook of Kyle's elbow.

"Hey, Penelope," he greeted back. "Did you hear what's happening tonight?"

"No," she replied, sounding interested. "Give me the deets."

"Well, let's just say we're going to see a show."

That was all I heard before the couple turned down the hall and their voices faded. I sighed and shifted around in my cage. If I was going to stay here for a while, I might as well try to get comfortable. Which was basically impossible, but hey, things could be worse, couldn't they?

I kept telling myself that.

In the silence, I tried summoning my magic. I'd never done magic in shifted form before, but surely it worked the same way, right? I focused on my body and honed in on my magic, but it was barely a tingle. Reciting the spell for healing in my head, I turned my focus to the end of my wings, which were still sore from the feather-plucking incident. The dull pain eased for a moment before it returned.

What the heck? When I couldn't perform magic back in Valkas's room, I'd assumed it was a *me* problem. But now here I was in the silence, all calm and ready to conjure magic, and it *still* didn't work?

A terrifying thought struck. Had Matias already used The Wise Owl?

No, not yet, I told myself. If he was blocking me, I wouldn't be able to shift.

Maybe I wasn't as calm as I thought I was, or perhaps I couldn't perform magic in shifted form, since I needed to speak the incantations out loud. Either way, magic wasn't going to get me out of this one.

Soon, more vampires emerged from the rooms lining the hallway, and I heard others I couldn't see and voices coming from the foyer. I didn't know how long I'd been in that cage, but judging by the sounds of the chateau coming alive, I had to guess that night had fallen.

After what felt like two hours since I woke, I finally saw a figure coming toward me down the hall. He had broad shoulders and took prideful steps.

Valkas.

He was flanked by three guards. I recognized the witch guy among them, but the other two were vamps. They all wore dark black, but their hands and faces were no longer covered. One of them had his sleeves rolled up, and I noticed the sign of the Soulless etched into his skin—a scar shaped like a V with two fang marks in the center.

Valkas stopped in front of me and peered down at me past his nose. "Well, shifter. I hope you're well rested. You have a big night ahead of you."

I didn't respond, seeing as I was in shifted form. But he probably would've slapped my head right off my shoulders if I actually spoke some snarky comeback.

Before I knew what was happening, Valkas grabbed the top of my cage, and I lost my balance. He swung the thing around as if there weren't a live being trapped inside. I slammed into one side of the cage only to be tossed to the other a split second later.

Take it easy, would ya?

Neither Valkas nor his men said anything. I was a little

disoriented trying to stay upright in the swinging cage, but I saw enough to know we were headed down the grand staircase. About a dozen vampires stood in the entrance chatting. They caught sight of Valkas and immediately went silent, bowing their heads at him while he passed. He didn't even acknowledge them, keeping his head high and eyes on the front door, like they were mere decorations.

Just before we slipped outside, I caught the eye of one of the women in the foyer.

Brown.

Her eyes were brown. It suddenly occurred to me that only half the people there were vamps. I didn't even have to look at their eyes in the dim lighting to know which ones they were. All the vamps stood close to their respective blood slaves, laying claim to them as if they were some piece of property.

The door swung shut behind us, blocking my view of the people inside. Outside, the sky was dark, and the air was cold. I couldn't see the stars behind the clouds, but the moon peeked through just enough that I could see the shadows of the trees.

I thought that maybe Valkas was taking me to the slaves' quarters. Maybe he'd show me off and use me as an example or something. But he veered in the opposite direction down a narrow path that led up a hill and toward the cliff.

It wasn't long before I heard the sounds of chanting. I couldn't make out the words, since there were various chants all going on at once, but it sounded like a bunch of people all getting psyched up before a big football game or something.

Valkas turned down a trail even narrower than the one we'd been on, then stopped when we reached a small clearing. In the middle of the clearing was a long wooden table with all sorts of weapons on it. I saw various types of knives, along with a sword, an ax, a bow and arrow, and even one of those chains with a spikey ball on the end.

What was this? Were they going to hold me down and fillet me or something?

Valkas set my cage down on the grass. Or rather, threw it. The cage landed upright but tipped over and rolled a few feet when my body slammed into the bars. He removed the keys from his pocket and bent to unlock the cage. He didn't even set it back upright before standing.

"Choose your weapon," he said, then he whirled around and started back down the trail. His men followed close behind him.

I quickly scurried out of the open cage, using my wings to hoist me out, then shifted.

"Wait!" I called before he could get too far.

Valkas paused, but when he turned and his men stepped aside so he could look at me, he didn't look pleased. Valkas wasn't the kind to take orders from anyone. I was pretty sure the only reason I was still alive was because he was curious to know what I had to say. Beneath the turned-down lips and narrowed gaze, I thought I detected a hint of amusement.

"Aren't you going to tell me what this is all about?" I asked, gesturing to the table of weapons. "Do I get to know what I'm up against?"

Valkas smirked, bringing all that amusement to the surface. "No, but that's the fun part."

"I don't even get a hint?" I protested. "How can I choose an adequate weapon if I don't know what I'm fighting?"

Valkas was upon me in a second. Wind rushed by my hair, and he reached out to smooth it down.

Ew! Don't touch me!

I tried not to let my detest for the man show, for my sister's sake.

"Pick the weapon that will do the most damage," he said coolly. "I'd very much like to see you survive the night."

"What?" My whole body went rigid. I wasn't scared to die. Not really. But I was scared of leaving behind unfinished business. That simply wasn't an option.

"Yes, darling," he said, taking note of my fallen face. "You're going to want to choose wisely. This one's a fight to the death."

7

A fight to the death? Was he serious? Against whom? Him? Another vampire? His witch crony? His hint wasn't exactly helpful, though he strolled away looking positively pleased with himself.

I turned back to the table, surveying the weapons under the moonlight.

I could run, I thought to myself. No one was around to see if I escaped into the forest. But then again, where would I go? Valkas had made sure I couldn't fly away, and I couldn't exactly swim to the mainland. I'd drown before I made it. Chances were the boathouse I'd heard about was heavily guarded after what had happened earlier. I'd never make it off this island before I was found, and Valkas didn't seem like the kind of guy who would forgive such an incident.

Which meant I was still playing his game, whether I liked it or not.

My eyes fell upon the bow, which had two arrows sitting next to it. That would be helpful for a long-distance shot, but

I'd never shot a bow before. There was a pretty good chance I wouldn't hit anything with it. I continued down the table, fingering the spear, then moving on to the sword. Most of these would kill a vampire, but what if I wasn't up against a vampire? Would I have to fight from close or far range? The chanting grew louder in the distance.

Just pick something, I told myself.

Without contemplating it too hard, I picked up the sword, which was heavier than it looked but would do a lot of damage. I grabbed one of the knives for good measure and slipped it in my boot.

Hey, Valkas never said anything about rules. He wanted a good show? I'd give him one.

A few moments later, I heard the sound of heavy footsteps approaching down the path. I whirled around with my sword held out in front of me, poised for attack.

A huge vampire stepped into the moonlight. He was at least six and a half feet tall with biceps bigger than my waist. He was shirtless, so I could see every hill and valley on his six-pack abs. I didn't care how much shifter blood I had in me. This guy would snap me like a twig.

He stopped at the entrance of the clearing and folded his arms over his chest. Interesting. I expected him to launch an attack right away.

"So, what's the deal?" I asked. "I attack, you rip my head off?"

Giant Vamp huffed and spoke in the deepest voice I'd ever heard. He spoke in a thick Russian accent, too. "If only it were easy. Come."

He turned back down the path, and it suddenly occurred to me. He wasn't my opponent. He was my escort. Clutching the hilt of the sword tightly in my hand, I hurried down the trail behind him. The guy's legs were super long, so it practically took me running to keep up with him.

"Any idea what I'm up against?" I asked, hoping for a little warning.

Giant Vamp scoffed. "Your opponent very fierce."

"Fiercer than you?"

The chanting grew louder as we walked. Up ahead, I saw lights flickering through the trees. *Torches*, I realized.

He smirked. "Nobody fiercer than Anton."

"Good to know. I'd hate to be the sorry loser fighting against you."

"Maybe one day," he said. "For now, you fight."

We reached a large clearing in the trees. I only had a moment to register the scene before me. Torches had been set into the ground, surrounding an empty square the size of a basketball court. The far end of the clearing met up with the edge of a tall cliff. I could barely see the water through the darkness, but I knew it was there. On either side of the torches sat people on raised bleachers, and beyond them, trees. The trees sloped down the hill, giving a wide view of the chateau.

There must've been at least two hundred people in the arena, which looked like a lot more all packed into the clearing. I couldn't tell if they were vampires or human, but my bet was most of them were vamps. Valkas sat in a big chair in the front row, like he was a king sitting on a throne, waiting for a jousting match to being. Rogers, the witch, sat at his side.

That was all I could process before Anton grabbed me by the back of the shirt and shoved me into the middle of the ring. I landed hard on my knees in the dirt, pinching my fingers between the hilt of my sword and the ground. I shot to my feet immediately, looking around for my opponent. Chants of *fight, fight, fight* filled the air, but I faced nothing but empty water at the other end of the ring. I whirled around to the trail entrance, but there was nothing there, either. Anton was already gone.

Valkas stood from his chair and held his hands up. The arena quieted without him having to give the command. It was eerily silent. The only thing I heard was the sound of the breeze rustling through the trees and the water against the rocks below the cliff.

"I'm sure by now you all know that we have a new shifter among us," Valkas said. He didn't speak loudly, as it was easy enough to hear him. I remained alert the whole time. "As with all our new recruits, she must be initiated."

Recruit? Is that what he was calling me? I didn't get any credit for finding this island when it was hidden beneath a cloaking spell?

I suppose not. He wouldn't want his loyal followers questioning his power.

"Only the strongest survive on my island." Valkas smirked at me. "So, without further ado, let the game begin!"

At his cue, a small creature flew out of the darkness as if someone had tossed it. It had gray fur and a long ringed tail.

A raccoon.

They thought I'd be afraid of this little thing? They obviously didn't know much about me.

It rolled across the dirt and immediately sprang to its feet when it came to a stop. An ax landed in the arena in the same manner, skidding to a halt beside the creature.

The raccoon lifted its gaze to mine, and an expression I

couldn't quite read crossed its features. I thought I detected a hint of surprise, but it quickly turned to fury. Something about that look seemed familiar, but I couldn't place it. The raccoon didn't even shift and grab its weapon before it sprang on me.

I ducked out of the way. The image of its tiny little paws reaching out for my face would forever be seared in my memory. The shifter landed on the ground behind me, clawing into the dirt to stop its momentum. It landed only a few feet away from the edge of the cliff.

I didn't want to hurt him. Killing humans and shifters wasn't my thing. I was all about slaying vampires. But I didn't want to die, either. The raccoon bared its teeth at me. Damn, it looked vicious. I had to make up my mind. And fast.

It lunged for me again, all while people screamed from the bleachers.

"Get her!"

"I wanna see some blood!"

"Use your sword!"

This time, I threw my hand outward and thrust it into the fur on the raccoon's chest. I followed his trajectory and spun around. I bent to one knee, using his momentum to slam his body into the ground. It earned me a round of applause.

I thought maybe if I got the shifter in the right position, we could talk something out—fake a death or something like that. He could go free, and I didn't have to kill him. It was a win-win for both of us.

But the little sucker didn't even hesitate. He gasped at the impact, then lifted his head and sank his teeth into my hand. I let out a yelp but didn't let go. I curled my fingers tighter in his fur, and he bit back harder. I bent down to his level, where blood dripped out of my palm and onto his fur. He used his little paws to scratch me, sending stinging shoots of pain up my hand.

"I'm trying to help you," I hissed. "Maybe there's a way we can both survive. You game?"

Instead of clawing at my exposed arm, he swiped his paw out and sliced across the skin on my cheek. I reeled backward.

"I'll take that as a no," I snapped back. I could barely hear my own voice above the cheering.

The raccoon bit down again, and I finally jerked my hand away. It hurt a lot, but the pain barely registered as my opponent righted himself and readied to jump at me again.

"Shift, shift, shift," the crowd cried out. I wasn't sure if they meant me or the raccoon. Either way, they wanted us to fight in the same form. No way was I shifting into a raven without my flight feathers. I was staying close to this sword the whole damn time.

I was ready for the next attack, but what I didn't expect was for the raccoon to shift mid-jump. A human body slammed into me, knocking me on my back. Another chorus of cheers broke out from the crowd. I held my sword up, but the shifter was already running away, heading for the other side of the arena to grab the ax. I jumped to my feet to see that the figure had short hair but a slim middle and wide hips. A woman?

Aw, shit. I really didn't want to kill her.

If you don't, she'll kill you, I told myself. And then there was no hope for getting rid of the vampires. I was the only one who could do it, and I'd do whatever it took until that happened. Even take innocent lives...

The thought made me sick, but it was what had to be done... for the greater good.

I hated when the greater good screwed you over.

I raced up to the woman just as she bent to grab her ax. She whirled around at the last second and moved so fast I didn't even see her face. The head of her ax clanged into my sword, knocking it out of my hands. Less than a split-second later, her fist swung out and slammed right between my eyes.

I stumbled to the ground, and my elbows skidded across the dirt. Judging by the sting, a good couple layers of skin came off. My vision blurred from the impact, but I wasn't ready to give up just yet. The girl stepped forward, her face masked in shadows.

"*Ardeat ignis,*" I shouted, aiming my hands at her. But all that came out was sparks.

It took me by complete surprise. Since learning the spell for fire, I hadn't had trouble using it in a fight. Now I'd failed at the spell twice? The theories I'd developed earlier about my magic no longer seemed credible. My latest theory, and worst of all, was that something was blocking my magic, something beyond my control.

Just another obstacle, I told myself. *I'll figure it out.*

Says the girl who lost her magical dagger, lost her ability to fly, and now lost her magic.

A heavy shoe connected with my gut. I grunted, and my arms instantly came to my abdomen, protecting from another blow.

Time for my back-up plan. I swung my leg out to connect with the back of the girl's ankle, then grabbed the knife out of my other shoe. She landed on her back on the ground, and her ax flew from her hand. The crowd shouted all sorts of things I couldn't process. I quickly scrambled to my feet and loomed above her, shoving the blade of my knife up against her throat.

Her face finally came into view. Shadows flickered across

it from the torches, but there was no denying that I'd seen that face a thousand times before. The straight nose, pale skin, blue eyes… they were all just like mine, only slightly tweaked.

All the air rushed out of my lungs. "Jenna?"

She smiled up at me. "Hey, sis."

8

____

I should've been overjoyed to see my sister, but all I could think was, *A raccoon! You never told me you were a raccoon!* Heck, I didn't even know she was a shifter! Then again, I'd never gotten the chance to tell her I was one, either. I guess I should've assumed as much.

"Jenna Bean?" I asked breathlessly.

Her hand shot out to grab on to my wrist, forcing the knife away from her throat. "What? You expected someone else, Rugrat?"

She spoke with such malice that I could hardly believe it was her. But there she was. Her hair was shorter, and she'd lost some weight, but it was definitely her.

"Yeah," I admitted. "I kinda did."

"Fight!" someone in the stands roared.

Jenna responded by slugging me hard on the inside of my arm, where she knew from many scuffles as children was my weak spot. I dropped the dagger on instinct. Mostly, I was just too shocked to fight back.

"What are you doing?" I demanded.

"Beating you up," she sneered. "What does it look like?"

Jenna's fist swung out again, connecting with the side of my jaw. The taste of copper filled my mouth. She jumped to her feet and readied herself for another blow.

"Jenna," I protested, still on my knees. "I'm not going to—"

Her foot slammed into my chest, knocking the air from my lungs. Seriously, what was her problem? Had the vamps messed her up that badly? Oh, God. What had they done to her?

That was all I could think as her fist connected with the side of my face again. Pain shot through my cheek, but I just couldn't bring myself to fight back. Everything I'd done, all the vampires I'd killed, had been for her. Suddenly, it felt like maybe there'd been no purpose in becoming the Ravenite. Maybe I shouldn't have come to Gregor Island at all.

"Jenna, stop!" I cried.

Her hands flew toward me again, but this time she didn't hit me. Instead, she fisted her hands in my shirt and pulled my face close to hers.

"I waited for you," she hissed. "For two damn years. Do you have any idea how long that feels when you're trapped on an effing island?"

"Jenna, I'm sorry—"

"Why didn't you come sooner?" she snapped, delivering another blow.

I barely felt it this time. I didn't care. I deserved it, because she was right. I should've come sooner.

"Because I—"

"Because you're selfish," Jenna bit, tossing me across the ground.

The momentum took me a mere foot from the edge of the cliff. I stole a quick glance at the steep drop, but I could barely process it. I was still trying to take in the fact that my sister was standing right in front of me after all this time. Jenna reached down and grabbed my clothes again, pulling me to my feet. She had a strong punch, and my eye was starting to swell because of it.

"Are you going to kill me?" I whispered. I loved Jenna more than anything in the world, but this wasn't the Jenna I knew. It broke my heart.

She heaved my body upward and slammed me to the ground. The sound of cheers grew so loud around me that I hardly heard what she said when she bent to whisper in my ear.

"No, I'm not going to kill you," she said. "Just play along. They like a good show."

"So, you're not really mad at me?" I asked in a raspy whisper.

She smirked. "Oh, I'm pissed. But we can discuss that later. Wanna punch me?"

No, not really, I wanted to say. The fact was, I'd rather hug her. But hey, what are sisters for? I curled my hand into a tight fist and swung it at her face.

Jenna let the momentum take her. She rolled to the side, clutching her cheek.

I should've felt bad about punching her, but I grinned like a lunatic. That punch to the face was proof that she was here. My sister was alive, and we were together again!

I threw myself at Jenna just as she was getting to her feet. My arm locked around her neck, and I held her in a headlock.

"What now?" I whispered in her ear while she clawed at my arm. "I won't kill you."

"Knock me out," she hissed.

"What? No."

"You want this to be over? Kick me in the face."

Punching her was one thing. Knocking her out was another. I didn't want her to end up with a concussion or something.

"I'll fake it," she said. "Do it now!"

Apparently, Jenna had developed a thing for pain since the last time I'd seen her. I swung my knee up just between her eyes, and her whole body went limp. I let her body fall to the ground, and the crowd went crazy. People shot up out of their seats, clapping and hollering.

I stared down at Jenna, horrified. For a moment, I thought I'd truly knocked her out. That kind of blow from a shifter could kill a human being, but surely Jenna would be okay. Right? *Right?*

She opened her eyes for a mere split second to wink at me. Relief flooded through me. I wanted to kneel beside her and drag her into a hug, but Valkas was already strolling out into the ring. He grabbed my hand in his—*shudder*—and held it above my head.

"Ladies and gentlemen," Valkas called, causing the crowd to quiet. "I give you your champion!"

The vampires went ballistic again.

"So, that fight to the death thing..." I said to him. "Just a rumor?"

Valkas smirked, as he always did. I was starting to wonder if it was a permanent expression. "Something like that. I'd have liked to see what would've happened if you took it seriously."

Valkas started toward the trail, and I had no choice but to follow him, seeing as he was still holding on to my hand. He gestured to Rogers, who immediately stood and followed behind us.

"What now?" I asked, glancing back at Jenna. She hadn't moved an inch. All the other vamps were starting to get up out of their seats, leaving her forgotten. "What about my sister?"

"Relax," Valkas said with a wave of his hand. "I wouldn't waste good shifter blood. She's too… sweet."

Repulsive! There was no doubt by the way he said it that he'd fed on her before. My heart ached for my sister. How was I going to get her away from here?

"Where are you taking me?" I demanded.

He tugged on my arm. "You ask too many questions, darling. From now on, I'll be the one asking questions."

"What kind of questions?"

I didn't even realize the irony until Valkas reacted. In the blink of an eye, his hand left mine, and it shot toward my throat. Instinct overtook, and I threw my arm up to block him. His face contorted with anger, and his other hand clamped around my neck as he shoved me hard up against a tree. My shirt rode up, and the bark skidded along my lower back, sending a raw pain across my skin. I couldn't breathe, but I didn't fight back, either.

Rogers just stood there observing, his hands folded in front of him. He didn't speak a word.

"I will not tolerate you taunting me," Valkas snapped. His face was only inches from mine, sending my heart pummeling against my rib cage. He lowered his voice and spoke in warning. "Your sister's blood can turn bitter *real* fast. So I suggest you don't make this a habit."

He wasn't lying. That much was clear. My sister's shifter blood couldn't protect her forever.

"Yes," I said in a raspy voice. It barely sounded like anything.

Valkas dropped me, and I inhaled a gulp of air. He grabbed me by the hand again and dragged me behind him before I could find my footing.

"Come," he snarled. "We must celebrate."

My stomach bottomed out. I didn't know what *celebrating* entailed, but there was something in his voice that suggested I didn't want to find out. Which meant I was still useful to him… for now.

I had to make sure it stayed that way.

9

Valkas led me back to the privacy of his room. The bed had been made, and the dagger he'd left on the desk was no longer there.

Rogers entered the room behind us and stood to the side. I swore the guy was just there for decoration. Which was crazy, considering he wasn't even that pretty. I mean, sure, he had the tall, muscular thing going on, but slicked-back hair was so not my style.

Valkas forced me to sit beside him on the bed. You'd think when a guy brought you back to his room, he'd be gentle about it and treat you like a lady, but it wasn't like that with Valkas. He practically yanked my arm out of the socket.

All I could think about was Venn, how he'd act like a gentleman if this were him.

Except Venn would never be in this type of scenario. He was too kind to run any sort of shifter fight club. And he *definitely* wouldn't bring a girl back to his room without asking.

Venn. I didn't know how much more heartbreak my body could handle, but I missed him so much.

Valkas leaned over to me, pressing his lips to the soft spot under my ear. My skin crawled, and nausea rolled around in my gut. All I wanted to do was pull away, but I didn't. There was still the whole *stay on his good side* thing… no matter how disgusted it made me feel. I'd never felt so sick in my life.

"Now that you've earned your place on this island," Valkas said, "there's something you should know about me."

You can't get it up? Let's hope to God, because if things went in that direction tonight, I didn't think Jenna and I were making it out of here. I'd die before I let the devil take my virginity. The greater good be damned.

I wasn't an expert on how vampire magic worked, but judging by some of the horndogs I'd run across during patrols, those parts still worked fine and dandy.

"Is he going to watch?" I gestured toward Rogers, who stood as still as a statue. His eyes were hard and looked untrustworthy. He took a job with the Soulless, for heaven's sake. I never trusted anyone with a heart black enough to side with vampires.

"What did I say about questions?" Valkas snarled.

"Right. Forgive me."

Valkas scoffed, like that was never going to happen. "No, darling. He's not here to watch. In fact, he's here to help."

I almost asked him to elaborate, but I clamped my mouth shut at the last second. Surely, that couldn't mean what it sounded like.

"You see, I'm very *particular* about my meals."

Meal? Well, that was better than other types of torture, but it still wasn't exactly a good thing. Being feed on was like being administered drugs you didn't want. It wouldn't kill you, but it was still a violation of your body.

Valkas pressed his lips to the underside of my jaw again.

This time, I actually did shudder. "I don't like my women… squirming."

At that, Rogers muttered the first words I'd ever heard come out of his mouth. *"Quod dico facies."*

My whole body went rigid, and panic tore through me. I tried to move, but my muscles wouldn't comply to my demands. It was like my whole body had gone to sleep, like my limbs weren't getting the signals that my brain was sending. What had that bastard done to me?

"Lie back," Valkas commanded.

Even if I wanted to, I couldn't move.

"Um…" Good to know my voice was still working.

"Shh," Valkas said, like I was some pet that needed soothing.

Rogers flicked his wrist, and I fell backward onto the bed. Fear ignited in my chest. If I had control of my body right now, I'd be shaking unlike ever before. For the first time, I wanted to beg for my safety. It was my last resort. Rogers had put me under some type of spell that turned me into his own personal marionette. How powerful was this creep?

"Don't worry, darling," Valkas said, looming over me. He reached up to brush a dark strand of hair out of my eyes, as if that was supposed to comfort me. It only made my heart pound harder—and definitely not in the good way. "This won't hurt a bit."

Valkas's fangs elongated, catching in the light of the burning sconce next to the bed.

"No, please—"

I gasped as Valkas's fangs sank into my neck. A sharp pain shot out across my skin, but was quickly replaced by a sense of euphoria. My heart rate instantly slowed, and a comforting warmth spread over my extremities like a soft blanket. My muscles relaxed, like I'd been immersed in a tub of calming potion.

I'd been bit once before, but that had lasted only a few seconds. It was easy to forget what it felt like after just the slightest taste. When Valkas fed on me, I felt so calm that I altogether forgot a vampire was stuck to my neck. I didn't think about the fact that I was trapped on this island. I didn't think about Jenna or Venn or my family. All that mattered was this feeling overtaking my body, like nothing could ever hurt me again.

I lost all sense of time. Valkas could've been feeding on me for a minute, or he could've been feeding on me for an hour. When he pulled away, I felt lightheaded and tired. I noticed him licking his lips but saw that there was no blood on them. He apparently wasn't a messy eater.

That was the only thought that went through my head before the reality of what had just happened hit me like a landslide. As soon as it registered, all the calmness I'd felt vanished. It was replaced by a dirty feeling beyond anything I'd ever felt before. I wanted to dive into a vat of chlorine and wash all the ickiness off of me.

I regained control of my body, and my hand slapped up to my neck. I wiped at the liquid there and pulled my hand away, expecting to see blood. But it was only saliva. Vampires could heal the wounds they inflicted with their saliva so that their prey didn't bleed out. I felt so woozy that I nearly forgot that tidbit of information.

I wanted to yell at Valkas, to tell him how wrong it was that he'd done that. But judging by the satisfied smirk on his face, he already knew how wrong it was.

I started to sit up, but Valkas placed a hand on my shoulder and pressed me back into the mattress. How could I have been so calm when he fed on me? This mattress felt like a rock.

"But darling," Valkas said. "We've only just begun."

Dear Lord. Don't tell me he was going in for another round. I didn't think I could handle any more blood loss. I felt like puking as it was, but maybe that was just from Valkas's close proximity.

Valkas lay beside me and propped himself up on his elbow. He twisted my hair around his finger while he spoke.

Gag.

"You are very sweet," he said. "Sweeter than your sister, even. It's a shame we hadn't met sooner."

Yeah, a real shame. I kept my lips sealed.

"Where were you that night?" Valkas asked, like we were old friends catching up.

"I don't know what you're talking about," I replied, careful not to phrase it as a question.

"That night your sister came to us."

My whole body tensed, and it wasn't from some puppeteer spell, either. He said it so casually, like he actually believed she made a choice coming with them. Maybe in his own twisted way, he did believe it.

"Oh? The night your men murdered my parents?" I couldn't help the question this time as my body shook in anger. Why would he bring that up? Was he trying to piss me off?

The thought of my parents punched an invisible hole through my gut. For so long, I'd avoided thinking about them. I pushed down the memory of their screams and their lifeless faces when I found them that night.

"My men?" Valkas asked innocently. "I think you mean *me,* darling."

He smiled as the blood drained from my face. There wasn't much left to begin with, so I could only imagine how pale I looked.

"You were there?" Another question. Dammit.

"Oh, yes." He gave me a cunning grin. "Who else could have murdered your parents in such a way?"

I squeezed my eyes shut, trying to shake the image from my mind. It'd been brutal and bloody beyond belief. I couldn't bear to recall the memory.

Now I was lying in bed with the man who'd murdered them. This couldn't be happening. I knew the Soulless had killed them, but I'd never known Valkas had been with them that night. I'd dreamed so many times of facing the man who murdered them, but in my mind, he always had a different face. In my head, it was always the guy with the scar above his eyebrow, the one who'd rampaged through my room while I hid in my raven form. I never truly thought I'd meet the vamp responsible.

"It's ironic," I said through clenched teeth, unable to keep my anger from rising to the surface.

"What is?" Valkas asked curiously.

I couldn't look at him. Instead, I stared straight up at the ceiling. "That you would be the one to take everything from me when I'm the only one who can kill you."

I finally looked at him, only to see his eyes narrow at me and his nostrils flare.

"It wasn't an accident," he snapped. Clearly, he didn't like being reminded that I was one of his biggest threats.

"I've been looking for you for a long time. As you know, you pose a threat to my existence, and I don't like feeling threatened." He leaned down to whisper in my ear, clipping each word. I held my breath. He pulled away a moment later, but it didn't seem soon enough. "Finding someone from an old life can be… tricky."

"I didn't know it was possible."

"Possible, for sure. But tricky. Luckily, Rogers here"—Valkas gestured to him in the corner—"came to the Soulless several years ago. He helped me track down the *young girl who could kill me.*"

"You must've offered him generous compensation." It was the only reason I could think of why a human would go along with this.

"One doesn't need compensation when they believe in the cause," Valkas drawled.

"And I suppose that cause is world domination."

"Ah, see?" Valkas said. "You already know me so well. We could get along, if only you wanted to be on the winning side."

"Oh, I do," I replied, finally looking him in the eyes. "I just don't intend for that side to be yours."

Valkas chuckled. "So naïve. I like it. And how do you intend to kill me when I have your dagger?"

I shrugged, feigning disinterest. "I haven't worked that one out yet."

Valkas grinned. "Excellent. Just what I like to hear."

"You tell a great story," I said, "but it doesn't make a lot of sense."

Valkas stiffened, like he was offended. "And how's that?"

"Well, you found me, but you took my sister instead."

Valkas drew away from me and pushed himself to a sitting position. I finally felt like I could breathe again. As soon as he stood, I sat up. Valkas passed by Rogers and headed to the table in the corner, where he poured himself a glass of an amber-colored liquid. I figured it was whiskey or something, but I didn't know why he was drinking it. It took a lot for a vamp to get a buzz. I think he just liked to hold the glass for something to do with his hands, like he thought it made him look intimidating or something.

Valkas took a sip and leaned casually against the table. "I don't admit to many mistakes, darling, but in my four hundred years, I have to say that was my biggest."

Before I could figure out how to phrase my question as a statement, Valkas continued.

"The fact is, we took the wrong girl." Valkas wore a pained expression, like it killed him to admit it.

I scooted myself to the edge of the bed so my feet hung off. It made me feel a little safer, like I could run if I had to. "So you tracked me down. You could've come after me again."

Valkas shrugged. "I could have, but Rogers counseled me to stay put, that you would come for me one day. And it seems he was right."

My gaze flickered to Rogers. "Witches can't see the future." Not without a magical object, at least. He couldn't have one, right?

Valkas took another sip, then gazed down into his glass, like there was something interesting in there. "It depends on how you look at it. Can they see a play-by-play of real events? No. But can they see generalities? Sometimes, if they're strong enough."

Answers to questions I'd been asking myself for years began to fall into place. "The Soulless disappeared two years ago, shortly after you took Jenna. Which means…"

I purposely let my statement run open-ended. I wanted him to confirm my suspicions without me having to ask.

Valkas spread his arms out wide. "Which means, it's all been for you, darling. I pulled back my men so that you'd come looking for me. I didn't know who you were until you conveniently showed up in my room."

So when he first mentioned Jenna, he was taking a wild guess, I theorized. It wasn't exactly hard to figure out we were sisters, considering our resemblance.

I swallowed down the lump in my throat. "Why are you telling me all this?"

Valkas crossed the room slowly, silently. He stopped in front of me, then his hand snapped out to crack across the side of my face. I let out a cry and brought my hand up to protect my cheek. It burned.

"What did I tell you about the questions?" he snarled. "You are such a curious shifter. The fact is, darling, honesty goes a long way."

That was saying a lot coming from the most morally corrupt man on the planet.

"You must figure that if you're honest with me, I'll tell you something in return," I guessed.

Valkas smiled, but it was one of the most gut-wrenching smiles I'd ever seen. I took that as a yes.

"You shouldn't have been so quick to show your hand," I said with a shrug. "Considering I don't have any secrets."

Valkas leaned closer to me, running a chilling finger down the side of my face. "Oh, but you do, darling."

"Funny," I deadpanned. "I don't seem to recall any."

Valkas sat beside me, and the mattress dipped under his weight. I could smell the alcohol on his breath. "I want to know what matters to you. *Who* matters to you."

I kept a stone-cold expression on my face as I looked him in the eye. "That's not a secret. You already know I care about my sister. I wouldn't be here if I didn't."

Valkas took another sip of his drink, then clicked his

tongue. "But two years, darling. That's a long time to be alone. I should know. I spent more than a century on this island. Didn't you meet anyone?"

"I met a handful of vampires," I said coolly. "But I never really got the chance to chat with them."

Valkas's lips turned up at the corners. "None of mine, I hope."

"None of your current followers, unfortunately."

Silence followed for a beat, then Valkas spoke. "So, what's your weakness, darling? A boy, perhaps?"

Venn! My body went rigid. I realized too late and hoped it didn't give me away.

"I have no one," I lied. The fact was, if I'd come here months ago, that would've been true.

"Darling," Valkas pouted, like he thought I might actually feel sympathy. "I was honest with you. It's only fair that you're honest in return."

"Fair?" I asked in disbelief. "You murdered my parents and kidnapped my sister. You want to talk about *fair*?"

I snapped my mouth shut. I didn't mean to snap at him, and it was probably a huge mistake. Soon, Valkas would get annoyed with my big fat mouth and shut it for me.

"You're right," Valkas said with a wave of his hand. He stood and set his empty glass on the nightstand. "There's no point in trying to be fair with you."

Valkas gestured to Rogers. Rogers reached into his pocket and pulled out a small vial with a clear liquid inside. He took a step forward and popped the top off.

"Whoa!" I cried, scurrying back across the bed. "Don't tell me you intend to give me that... whatever it is."

"Oh, I absolutely do," Valkas said with an evil smile.

Rogers reached out for me, but I pulled my arm away.

"But you didn't tell me what's in it," I protested.

Valkas raised an eyebrow. "I'm not obligated to. You'll take the potion, or I'll force you to watch as I carve your sister's skin off."

For a moment, I had forgotten how cruel Valkas was. He was playing nice with me, which made him almost seem... human. But he was only doing it to manipulate me, and when he realized that wasn't working, he was right back to his devilish antics.

"What is it?" I asked.

Big mistake. Valkas was *so* done with my shit at this point. He jumped on the bed and slammed his hand into my chest. I fell back onto the mattress, and he climbed on top of me, holding me down. I squirmed beneath him, trying to break free. What if it was some sort of poison that would kill me? Or a potion that would prevent my soul from reincarnating?

I threw my hands up to his face, but he grabbed on to my wrists and squeezed tightly, holding them above my head. I fought against him, but I was so weak from the loss of blood that it didn't do anything.

"Now!" Valkas roared.

Rogers reached out for my face. I snapped at his hand with my teeth and tasted blood. Valkas readjusted his hands to squeeze the corners of my jaw and force my mouth open. Rogers tipped back the vial, and a tasteless liquid entered my mouth. I planned to spit it out, but Valkas forced my jaw closed, and Rogers pinched my nose shut. My lungs felt like they were going to implode. Basic instinct took over, and I swallowed the liquid against my will.

My body went still. It wasn't like when Rogers tried to go all *puppet master* on my ass. Nor was it like the calmness that overcame me when Valkas fed on me. This was more or less like I'd given up fighting. Which was *so* unlike me. Whatever they'd given me acted quickly. Rogers returned to his post at the door, and Valkas sat beside me on the bed.

He spoke slowly. "I'm only going to ask one more time. Besides your sister, what other weaknesses do you have?"

"My family," I admitted. I had no idea where the words came from, but I felt them slip out of my mouth, heard them come in my own voice.

Truth potion! The bastard.

"Ah," Valkas said in interest. "Tell me more."

I found myself spilling every last detail about Venn, Fiona, and the rest of them. I told Valkas about how I'd met them, what their powers were, and how I felt about each and every one of them.

Truth be told, I couldn't remember much of what I said beyond that. I wasn't sure if I was still feeling woozy from the blood loss or if it was part of the potion that made my head fuzzy. Either way, secrets tumbled out of my mouth that I never would've told Valkas otherwise. Eventually, he took my hand and guided me up off the bed. My knees shook, and the room spun around me. I felt drunk, only without the urge to vomit. Which was weird, because Valkas constantly made me nauseous.

He led me toward the door, but before he let me go, he leaned over to whisper in my ear. "In case it wasn't clear, darling, that's how I expect you to act every time I ask you a question. I'm done giving you second chances. I expect nothing but respect from now on." Valkas straightened and turned to Rogers. "Deal with her."

Valkas let me go, and it was enough to send me falling to my knees without the support. A pair of hands reached out and caught me, then I felt my body being tossed upward. It took me a second to realize I was slumped over someone's shoulder and already headed down the hall.

"Where are you taking me?" I thought I asked the question, but I didn't hear the words come out.

"Shh…" It was hard to pinpoint the voice, but I thought it was Rogers. "You mustn't worry."

He was dead wrong about that. Worry was all I did these days.

It certainly wasn't going to end now.

10

It was dark when I blinked my eyes open. I shot to a sitting position, but the top of my head slammed against something hard. I rubbed the goose egg on my head and cursed.

"Rachel," a familiar voice called out from the darkness.

"Jenna?"

My eyes adjusted to the darkness to see that I was in one of the log cabins the blood slaves stayed in. Light from an oil lamp cast shadows across the room. I was lying on a lower bunk, and Jenna was eyeing me from the bunk opposite mine. Two other girls who looked a few years older than me gazed down with sad eyes from the bunk above Jenna.

Everything that had happened since I arrived at Gregor Island came rushing back. My skin crawled at the memory of what had happened in the privacy of Valkas's room. All I wanted to do was take a shower. My stomach rumbled, and I realized I was starving. My arms shook as I pushed myself up to sit on the edge of the bed.

"I'm glad you're okay," I said.

Jenna forced a smile. "For now. As long as they think they can use me to manipulate you."

Of course. That's why Valkas hadn't let her die in the ring.

"What happened?" I asked.

Jenna cleared her throat. "Rogers dumped you at our door, said you were our new roommate. This is Andi and Bri, by the way."

I looked up to the girls on the top bunk. One had long blond hair and a small nose, and the other had dark skin and tight curls. Judging by the way they were sitting, they looked close, like being on this island had brought them together.

"Hey," the blonde waved.

"Hi." I gave a non-committal smile.

"Are you okay?" Jenna asked, eyeing me with concern, a look I'd seen so many times throughout the years.

"Just hungry," I lied.

"What happened to you?" she asked.

I dodged around the question. I'd rather talk to her in private. "Is there anything to eat around here? Or anywhere to shower?" I added.

Jenna stood. "Follow me."

"Hey," the dark-haired girl said softly, stopping her. "You want us to come with?"

"We'll be fine, Andi," Jenna answered. "But thanks for the offer."

Jenna and I stepped out of the cabin into cool night air.

I turned to her. "So, you've still got some of that softness in you?"

Jenna frowned. "A lot has changed since we last saw each other, but I'm not a monster."

"Huh. Could've fooled me," I said, recalling her fist flying toward me in the ring.

Her shoulders dropped. "Come on, Rachel. Don't be like that. I didn't mean what I said. I was shocked and overwhelmed. I wasn't sure I actually believed it was you."

I was just about to shoot back some snarky comment, but then I looked her in the eyes. All my snark vanished as tears rose to my eyes. Out here alone under the moonlight, it felt like I was seeing her for the first time since the night she was taken. And I lost it.

Without ceremony, I threw my arms around her neck and dragged her close. She still smelled like I remembered... subtle tones of fresh linen mixed with a light strawberry scent. Memories of us as kids rushed through my mind—playing in our treehouse pretending we were pirates, talking about boys at our late-night slumber parties, baking cookies with Mom at Christmas, and grilling out with Dad in the summertime. Tears rolled down my cheeks. Once they started, I couldn't turn them off. Jenna hugged me back, and for the first time since I'd lost her, I felt that hole inside my chest shrink ever so slightly.

"I'm so sorry," I whispered, my voice cracking. "I'm sorry I didn't come for you sooner."

Jenna drew away from me and wiped at her eyes. The tough exterior she'd put up earlier in the night had completely crumbled. "Where were you, Rachel? I waited for you. I thought they'd killed you that night. I kept telling myself they didn't, that you were alive and coming for me. But I-I—"

I sniffled. "I tried, but I didn't know where to start. I was hopeless. Once I had enough money, I turned to a witch and tried to track you down, but the spell didn't work. I didn't know what else to do, so I gave up. I'm a horrible sister. I didn't think I had a chance of finding you until I saw this vampire with the mark of the Soulless on his wrist. That changed everything. I finally found out where you were, but then… shit hit the fan."

Jenna took my arm and led me toward a large building at the end of the rows of cabins. A few people passed by, but the cabins were mostly quiet. "Why don't you tell me about it inside? Let's get you cleaned up."

We stepped inside a dark building with rooms going off in all different directions. It was stylized in the same way as the cabins, with smooth wood floor and thick wooden walls. Jenna led me into one of the first rooms. I could hardly see anything until she turned to a table next to the door and lit a match. She placed it to the wick of an oil lamp, and the room became cast in a soft glow. I looked around to see three separate tubs, the kind on claw feet, with hand-pump faucets over each of them.

"No running water?" I asked.

Jenna walked over to the nearest tub and set the lamp down on an end table next to it. "Unfortunately, no. The island is completely cut off from the mainland. Valkas has a few generators here and there, but he saves them for himself. Get in. I'll pump your water for you."

I stood at the head of the tub and hesitated.

"Come on," Jenna encouraged. "We're sisters. We used to take baths together as kids. It's nothing I've never seen before."

True. I stripped down and climbed into the tub while Jenna worked on the pump. Icy cold water rushed over my toes, and I screamed, almost jumping out of the tub.

Jenna laughed. "No electricity, either. Remind me again what a warm shower feels like."

"A lot more pleasant than this." I settled back down into the tub, trying to ignore the coolness surrounding me.

When Jenna looked at me with her soft blue eyes, I could see the sister I used to know. She spoke quietly. "Do you want to tell me about it now?"

Yes! I wanted to tell her everything.

I took a calming breath, then dove into everything that happened after I found out about Gregor Island. I told her all about being the Ravenite, about Clarita's warning, about our journey to the caves and my encounter with Matias. I told her about the dagger, my past lives, Synchrony, Venn—all of it. By the time I'd finished, I was clean and had been soaking in the tub for what felt like an hour.

"Wow," Jenna said, dragging out the word. She sat on the lip of the next tub, her elbows rested on her knees. "That's... a *lot* to take in."

I bit my lip. "I know. I think I know what Clarita's warning meant now."

She tilted her head in question.

"Her warning was all about the dagger. If I hadn't gone down into the cave, I'd never would've faced Matias. I never would've gotten the dagger that could kill Valkas. But now..." I dropped my head. "I messed up, Jenna Bean."

She sighed, like she didn't know what to say. She had no words of comfort to offer me.

"You're a big help, sis," I stated flatly.

Her shoulders fell. "What do you want me to say, Rachel? That you can't give up? That you'll make it off this island alive? I've been here a long time, and I've never seen anyone escape. This is our reality now."

My stomach felt hollow. This couldn't be it, could it?

But Jenna had a point. We didn't have a way off this island. My one chance had already come and gone, and I didn't know what to think about that. *Hopeless* was the best way to put it.

To take my mind off it, I asked Jenna, "So, what's up with this island anyway? How'd a chateau end up out here? I mean, if this place was hidden for over a century…"

"As far as I've heard, the mansion was here before Valkas was imprisoned. The cabins and stuff only came after he escaped. His cronies run off to the mainland all the time to bring supplies back."

"So, the Soulless… are they all here, then?" I'd honestly expected there to be more of them.

"God, no," Jenna answered. "The Soulless are everywhere, stationed at different places around the world. This is just their headquarters, where Valkas keeps the strongest of them and the ones he trusts most."

"Oh, okay." It made sense.

"Anyway, about the mansion… rumor has it one of the witches who trapped him here—Gregor, obviously…" She shot me a knowing look, since I'd told her all about my past lives. "Lily Gregor owned the island and lived here on and off. She offered it up as the place of his sentence. As the legend goes, the mansion was symbolic to his imprisonment. It was supposed to make him reflect on what he'd done, to look at all the empty rooms and think of the people he'd killed."

I laughed lightly.

"What?" she asked curiously.

I shrugged. "That sounds like something I'd come up with, even if it was in a past life."

"I still can't believe you're all those people." She spoke so softly I barely heard her. "It's crazy that my sister is such an important part to all of this."

"It's not like I chose it," I said.

"I know, but…" Jenna left the sentence hanging. The following beat of silence made me a little uncomfortable.

"I still can't believe you're a raccoon," I subbed in, laughing.

Jenna smirked. "What did you expect? A dragon?"

I smiled. "I guess I always knew you'd be a shifter. I mean, since it's genetic and all of that. But I just couldn't ever picture you as an animal, you know? I mean, you're *Jenna*."

"Jenna the Fierce Raccoon," she teased. "And don't you forget it."

"Oh, I won't be forgetting that anytime soon."

"And you're a raven?" She rose her eyebrows, like she was impressed. "Can't say I'm surprised. I think it suits you."

"Does it?" I asked. I didn't know what that meant, but I supposed it did, in a way.

Another beat passed, but I spoke to break the silence. I was dying for more details. "What happened to you these last two years?" After a pause, I added, "Only if you want to talk about it…"

Jenna shrugged, like she didn't mind sharing. It was weird. I looked at her, and she was my sister, but there was definitely something tougher about her than I'd ever seen before. I guess that was what being a blood slave did to you.

She laced her fingers together in front of her. "What's there to tell? I was kidnapped, fed on, and forced to fight other shifters for the vampires' sick entertainment."

My stomach dropped like a bag of rocks. I hated that she'd gone through all of that. "That's how you got so good at fighting?"

"I had to," she answered coolly. She barely sounded like my sister when she talked about it. "They care about shifter blood around here—for feeding—but they care about watching a good show, too. Some of those fights end in death, Rachel."

I knew they had to, but hearing it from her mouth made me shudder.

"I've done what I had to do to survive," she said, not meeting my gaze. "I didn't always want to, but…"

"But what?" I regretted asking the question as soon as it left my lips. I didn't want to make Jenna say any more than she was comfortable with. I understood how hard this kind of thing was to talk about.

"But I wanted to survive. To see you again."

Tears rose to my eyes again. She endured all that for me?

"I love you, Jenna," I whispered.

"I love you, too, Rach. Now finish up." She stood and turned away from me, but I heard her sniffle as she paced across the room. It was like she didn't want me to see her cry. Wow, how she'd changed.

I scrubbed down a second time to give her a moment of privacy. She handed me a towel when I got out, but didn't say anything. I dried off, enjoying the warmth that came with it, then wrapped the towel around my body and secured the corner under the pit of my arm. I gathered my clothes and folded them into a neat pile, then took a bar of soap. Jenna eyed me curiously.

"You know how I told you I was a witch?" I asked.

"Like I could forget that." She rolled her eyes playfully.

I smirked. "Do you want to see me perform magic?"

Genuine interest crossed her features. "Yes!"

Jenna and I settled on the floor on either side of my pile of clothes. I held the bar of soap above the clothes and whispered the cleansing incantation Sondra had taught me.

"Did it work?" Jenna asked when I finished.

"Wasn't very fantastical, was it? It's one of the only spells I know." I grabbed my shirt off the top and sniffed it. It had a hint of the soap scent hidden beneath a layer of sweat, as if the spell had only half worked. My shoulders fell. "This worked perfectly the last time I used it."

Jenna sniffed my jeans. "Ew, Rachel."

My eyebrows knitted together. "I know. This spell is simple. It's like ever since I stepped foot on this island something's been blocking my powers."

Jenna pressed her lips together in thought. I could barely see her expression in the shadows.

"What?" I asked, seeing the gears turning in her head.

"I'm just thinking about what you told me about Synchrony. You talked about positive and negative energy."

"I do have positive energy," I countered. "I've been getting a lot better at casting spells. How can all of that just go away?"

"Because that's how life works," Jenna said. "Nobody's positive all the time, Rachel. Sometimes, it takes just one thing to set us back ten spaces."

I snorted. "One thing? Like Valkas."

"Exactly," Jenna agreed. "Magic isn't a linear progression. It's a rollercoaster ride of loops and turns and ups and downs."

A light smile crossed my lips. "When did you become the expert in magic?"

Jenna shot back a smirk. "I'm not. I just know how life works. I've been through enough shit to know that one."

I dropped my gaze, really contemplating what Jenna was saying. "Maybe you're right. I have been holding on to a lot of anger lately." I closed my eyes and took a deep breath, trying to force out some of the tension in my shoulders.

"Believe me…" Jenna reached out and placed her hand on mine. I opened my eyes to look at her, and the rest of the tension melted out of me. Her words were like an energy of their own, reminding me that I wasn't alone. "I know how hard it is to stay positive in the roughest moments."

Silence settled over the washroom as Jenna and I stared at each other. The knot in my chest softened, and I felt my lips twitch into a smile. I turned my hand over to hold on to hers. Jenna didn't have to say anything else. Just her presence here and the familiar look in her eyes restored a sense of peace within myself I realized I'd let slip away.

"Can you try the spell again?" she asked.

"Okay." I grabbed the soap bar and repeated the incantation. This time, my clothes smelled fresher, though they still had a few dirt stains on them.

Jenna shrugged. "Good enough, I guess."

I changed back into my clothes and ran my fingers through my hair. Before Jenna and I left the building, I stopped her. "Hey, Jenna?"

She paused with her hand on the doorknob. "Yeah?"

"Don't let me forget what you said, okay? About the ups and the downs. I need a reminder about that every now and then."

She draped an arm around my shoulder and opened the door. "Me, too, sis. Me, too."

11

I laid my head back in the sand and closed my eyes, focusing on the sound of the waves lapping against the shore. The sun was hidden behind a thick layer of clouds, as it tended to do here on Gregor Island. I thought that maybe the sounds of nature would take my mind off everything, but it did nothing to shrink the gaping hole in my chest where all the hope and determination I'd had once resided. Now, there was nothing.

Several days had passed, but it felt like months. I still wasn't any closer to figuring out how to find that dagger, kill Valkas, and get off the island. At this point, I didn't think I ever would.

On the bright side, I hadn't seen Valkas again, which was both a good and a bad thing. On one hand, I didn't *want* to see him again. On the other, it made me a little suspicious. I'd stayed alive that first night because he was having fun with me. Now he was totally ignoring me? It didn't sit right with me, but I decided to look at it as a blessing.

Blessings these days were few and far between. I spent my

nights forced into slave labor in the chateau, cleaning chimneys and fireplaces or polishing baseboards. That part wouldn't have been so bad if it weren't for the uniform, a tight-fitting outfit that my butt cheeks hung out of. At least once an hour some sicko would pass by and whistle at me. I'd even been slapped in the ass a few times—and I just took it, because what was the point in fighting back now?

During my downtime, I'd been trying to channel more positive energy, but it wasn't helping with my magic. It was nigh on impossible to stay positive after everything I'd seen.

I watched a female vampire grope her male blood slave in front of his cabin, squeezing so tightly that tears rose to his eyes. Then she criticized him for showing any emotion, saying he should be pleased because they "always had a good time." I listened to a woman cry in the next cabin over after she returned from a feeding, and I saw a man beg a vamp for a feeding, just to get that high from it he'd become addicted to. The vamp refused and looked positively pleased when the man fell to his knees and begged for a hit.

One guy even went into shock from blood loss on his way back from the chateau, and a group of blood slaves had to carry him back to the cabins and nurse him back to health. His master forced him back on his feet the next evening.

The second night I was here, I listened to the story of how Andi had been snatched the night before her wedding a few months ago, straight from the hotel suite her maid of honor had booked for the bridal party. I felt sick each morning Jenna returned from the chateau after being paraded around and fed on. The life in her eyes left for a good two hours afterward until she finally felt like talking again.

I tried not to let it all get to me, but I couldn't force the nausea out of my gut. Instead, I figured I could use it to fuel my power, shaping the anger and resentment I felt toward the vampires into love and compassion for their slaves.

"*Ardeat ignis.*" A blast of flames shot up out of my palm, but as soon as it came, it was gone.

All my efforts were futile. I rolled over in the sand and pulled my knees up to my chest, curling into a ball. This wasn't the first time I'd ever given up, but somehow, it felt like it would be my last. Valkas was planning something for me. I was sure of it. Soon enough, he was going to get bored of keeping me around. I'd already lost so much. I didn't have long before I'd lost absolutely everything, including Jenna.

"That fire was sweet."

I started at the sound of the voice behind me and sat up. "Jenna."

She plopped down in the sand and bumped her shoulder against mine. "It was really cool. You should do it again."

I shook my head. "It's not working right. I don't know if it's me, or if it's something about this island. Probably me."

It was like Synchrony had forgotten about me, like I was no longer needed and Synchrony wasn't willing to respond to me anymore.

"Nothing's gone as planned," I continued. "It feels like I'm just sitting around waiting for Valkas to sink my teeth into me."

Jenna laughed. "Aren't we all?"

I shrugged, totally not feeling the laughter right now. I dropped my gaze to the sand and curled my arms around my knees. It felt like I had to shrink into a ball just to hold myself together, like if I stretched out, my guts would fall right out of my abdomen.

"What are you doing out here?" I asked. "Shouldn't you be sleeping?" The whole island went to sleep during the day.

Jenna rolled her eyes. "Screw that. It's the only time any of us get to ourselves."

I looked away without responding.

Her expression turned serious. "Are you okay?"

Tears pricked at my eyes, and my throat swelled. I bit my lower lip to hold it all back, but I couldn't keep it from Jenna. "No," I admitted, my voice cracking. "I'm not. I—"

I wanted to explain it all to her, but the words wouldn't come out. Instead, tears began rolling down my cheeks. I buried my face into my knees, letting the tears soak into the jeans Jenna had leant me.

"Rachel," she whispered.

She placed a gentle hand on my shoulder, and I lost it. My shoulders heaved against my will, and I turned into a blubbering mess. Once it started, I couldn't turn it off. Jenna scooted closer to me and wrapped an arm around my shoulder. She didn't say anything. She just stroked her fingers through my hair, then ran a comforting hand across my back.

I leaned into her and cried until my tears dried up. Soon, my sobs turned into dry heaves.

It'd been up to me to rid the world of the vampire curse, and I'd let everyone down. All the terrible things the vampires did… the murders, the feedings, the abuse… it would all go on without any way to stop it. Is that what Synchrony wanted?

If so, Synchrony was stupid.

Then there was Venn, Fiona, and the rest of them. I'd never see them again. They'd never know what had happened to me. I wished I could tell them how sorry I was.

"Do you want to talk about it?" Jenna finally whispered.

I buried my face deeper into her shoulder and shook my head. Even though I objected to her invitation, I found myself speaking anyway. "I feel like such a screw-up."

"You're not a screw-up," she argued.

"I am," I cried, lifting my head. I wiped at my face. "I was the key to making the world a better place, but I totally screwed it up. I don't have a chance of getting that dagger back. I'll never kill Valkas, and we'll never make it off this island."

Jenna's eyes glistened with tears. Damn it. I was going to start bawling again if she cried.

"I can't stand to see you like this," she whispered.

"Then go away," I offered.

"No! I'm not leaving you alone at a time like this."

"It's fine, Jenna. I'll be all right." It was a total lie. All I wanted was to be next to her.

"You're my sister," she said. "And what should sisters do?"

Her words caught me off guard. It was something Mom always said when Jenna and I were fighting. She'd force us to look each other in the eyes and would say those exact words.

"Sisters shouldn't fight," Mom would tell us.

"Yeah, yeah," we'd reply in unison.

Mom would come back in a stern voice and say, *"What should sisters do?"*

"Love each other," I answered.

Jenna nodded. "That's right. You better believe it when I say it. I *love* you, Rachel. And I'm here for you."

I forced a smile. "Thanks, Jenna."

"For what?"

"For your positive energy. I don't know how you've kept it all this time. I wouldn't be nearly as strong as you if I went through what you have these last couple of years."

"Kept it?" she repeated. "Rachel, I *make* my own positive energy. You don't survive long on this island without it. No

one's going to hand that to you here. You have to go make it yourself. Ups and downs, remember?"

I considered her words for a moment, then said, "When did you get so wise?"

Jenna laughed. "I've always been this wise, dweeb. It took you long enough to notice." She got to her feet and held out an inviting hand. "Follow me. I want to show you something."

All I wanted to do was stay here and shrivel up, but Jenna had me intrigued. Curiously, I took her hand and followed her into the woods.

"Where are we going?" I asked as we stepped over fallen logs and underbrush.

"It's not very far," she replied, but she didn't answer my question.

After a short hike, Jenna came to a stop beside a large rotting stump. A thick log lay on the ground beside it, which was covered in a large pile of sticks and other debris. She sat on the ground beside it and looked up at me.

"What is this?" I asked.

She patted the dirt next to her. "I've never shown anyone this before, so you'll have to keep it a secret."

"Who am I going to tell?" I lowered myself beside her.

She shrugged. "True."

"So, what's the secret?"

She took a deep breath. "You asked me how I stay positive. The truth is, it's not easy. Honestly, I'm not sure if I'd even use that word—*positive*. The fact is, I gave up a long time ago. I resigned myself to the fact that the Soulless had taken everything from me and there was no way to get any of it back."

Sounds familiar.

"About four months in, someone said something to me. He

told me, *'The Soulless can take everything from you—except for who you are.'*

She paused for a moment to let the words sink in. Honestly, I wasn't quite sure what she meant. It sure seemed like the Soulless could strip you of everything if they wanted to.

"That stuck with me, but it wasn't until I made this that I started to understand what it meant." Jenna pushed the debris aside and pulled out a hand-made wreathe from beneath the pile. "I couldn't change what the Soulless did to me. I could only change how I reacted to it."

I took the wreathe in my hands to examine it. It was made of twisted evergreen boughs, with pinecones and acorns attached. "You made this?"

Jenna nodded. "For Mom. I know it's silly, but I just had to make her one."

"For Mother's Day," I said breathlessly. Jenna and I always made one together for her.

She pulled out a second one to show me. This one was bigger and more intricate and had dried flowers scattered throughout.

"I can't believe you still make her a wreathe every year."

Jenna smiled shyly. "I made you something, too."

"You did?" I looked up at her in shock.

She pulled out a long, hollow stick that had a line of holes cut out along its length. "It's supposed to be a flute."

I took it and handed her back the wreathe. I could hardly find the words. "You really made this for me?"

"Yeah, for your eighteenth birthday. I never thought I'd get the chance to give it to you, though. I thought that maybe I could use it to play that lullaby Mom used to sing to us."

"The full moon is shining. The stars glitter above," I sang softly.

"The wind whispers softly, 'Goodnight, my love,'" Jenna finished.

Now my eyes were tearing up for an entirely different reason. I brought the flute to my lips and blew through it. Nothing happened.

Jenna giggled. "It didn't work out like I'd hoped."

My lips lifted at the corners. "Thank you anyway. It's a really sweet gift."

Silence passed between us, but it was anything but awkward. It felt good to just sit here with my sister. It'd been so long. I forgot how nice it was.

Finally, Jenna took a deep breath and spoke. "Anyway, I came down to the beach because I wanted to talk to you about something."

"Oh?"

She took the flute back and placed everything beneath the debris pile again, where it was hidden from view, then turned to me. "I've been doing some thinking. For so long, I honestly thought I'd never see you again, and now here you are. You know what that tells me?"

I shook my head.

"Even when we've given up hope, there's still a chance. I'm starting to think that maybe this isn't the end."

"Really?" I asked, my heart lifting slightly.

"Really."

My stomach dropped. She was talking crazy.

"How am I going to get the dagger back?" I asked. "I don't even know where it is."

Jenna pressed her lips together in thought. "I think I know someone who can help us. Are you up for a party?"

"A party?" That sounded like something we'd get in trouble for.

Jenna waved her hand nonchalantly. "The vamps don't care what we do as long as we're at their side when they say so. Personally, I think they let us have our little bits of freedom because they know we'll comply easier with it. The feedings aren't as bad if you have something to look forward to afterward. Not to mention healthier blood slaves taste better."

Ew! The thought made me cringe.

"I swear it's the only thing that keeps me from going crazy," she said. "And I'm sure that's why they let you room with me. So… are you up for it?"

I hesitated. "What kind of party?"

"Just some people getting together down at Eagle Rock."

"Will there be booze?"

Jenna laughed. "Do you think the Soulless wouldn't supply alcohol? Alcohol-infused blood is the best kind."

"It's stupid and reckless," I told her.

"Yep." She patted my knee for show. "And that's one good thing about me that hasn't changed. What about you, Rugrat?"

I guess it wouldn't hurt to let loose a little—since I was stuck here anyway. "I do reckless shit all the time. What do you think brought me here?"

"Awesome. Is that what you're wearing?"

I tugged at the hem of my shirt. "Is there a dress code?"

Jenna stood and held her hand out to me. "Come on. Let's go find you something."

12

"**D**amn, you look hot!" Jenna whistled from across the cabin.

I twirled around to show off the black bikini from all angles.

"When did you get boobs?" she teased.

I swatted at her. "Shut up. I've always had them. Where'd all these clothes come from, anyway?"

She shrugged, glancing to the dresser at the foot of her bed. "I don't know. The vampires supply them. They're all enchanted to shift with us, too."

"That's weird," I said. "It's almost like they care."

She rolled her eyes. "Don't be so naïve, Rachel. Would you let *your* pet run around in rags all the time?"

I frowned at the word *pet*. It was sick that that was all she was to them.

"How does it work?" My tone shifted, becoming soft, and I sank down onto the bottom bunk beside her. "With the vamps, I mean. Do they… share you?"

"No," Jenna replied with a shake of her head. She dropped

her gaze and picked at her fingernails. "Each of the Soulless has one or two blood slaves specific to them. The higher up in the rankings they are, the more they get. Of course, Valkas gets his choice of any of us, but he cycles through his favorites."

"And you...?" I started hesitantly.

"I used to be one of his favorites," she answered with a frown. "But he gets bored easily. I've been with Silas for about a year. He's gentler than Valkas, but..."

"But what?" I pressed.

She sighed. "But it's unpleasant."

"Yeah. No one's exactly begging for vampires to go around biting them."

"Oh, believe me," Jenna said, "some people do."

An uncomfortable silence hung in the air. I quickly changed the subject. "So, that day I came here, when Valkas ripped that guy's heart out, where were you? I thought I'd find you up at the chateau, but..."

"No, I was actually down on the beach. I was lucky enough not to witness that."

"The beach?" I suddenly remembered seeing a couple sitting down there while I was flying over the island. Jenna's hair was shorter, and she'd put on some muscle since the last time I saw her, so I hadn't recognized her from above. "Who was that guy you were with?"

She shot me a confused expression, as if to ask how I knew. Then she stood and started for the door. "Come on, Rach. There's someone I want you to meet."

I followed behind her in bare feet along one of the trails. Laughter broke through the trees, and I heard the sound of water splashing in the distance. It wasn't long before the forest opened and I saw a group of people gathered where the trail ended. Jenna and I stepped out onto a wide, rocky surface that rose about fifteen feet out of the water. Moss and grass covered the ground, and a tall tree hung over the edge of the rock, where a guy in swim trunks was swinging from a rope. He let go and flailed his arms as he plummeted toward the water. People around him cheered and clapped.

"Hey, Jenna!" A guy holding a beer approached us. He had six-pack abs, long blond hair tied into a bun at the base of his neck, and a small amount of facial hair on his chin. He looked like a hippie, but a sexy hippie.

"Hey, Ronark," Jenna greeted, gesturing to me. "This is my sister, Rachel."

"A pleasure," he said, extending his hand out to me.

"Call me Rae," I said, shaking his hand. "So, Ronark? That's an interesting name."

"It's a surname," he said. "Elijah just doesn't sound as cool, you know?"

"I think Elijah is a good name," I told him.

Ronark laughed. "You wanna take your chances on the rope, Rae?"

I glanced over to the girl doing a backflip off of it. It actually looked kind of fun.

I shrugged. "Sure, why not?"

"You have to play the game, though," he insisted.

"Okay, I'm intrigued. What's the game?"

"It's a variation of Truth or Dare," Jenna explained. "If you step up to the rope, you have to do whatever challenge the person behind you gives you, or you don't get to go again. We go until there's only one person left."

I smirked. "Challenge accepted."

I stepped up to the line behind a girl with dark skin and shoulder-length black hair. Ronark took the spot behind me, with Jenna behind him. The dark-haired girl glanced back at me after grabbing the rope.

"You have to give her a dare," Ronark explained.

"Um, okay…" I thought about it for a moment. "No using your legs?"

She smirked. "Easy."

She held high up on the rope, took a running start, and jumped off the end of the rock. She went soaring through the air and pencil-dived feet-first into the water.

The rope came swinging back to me, and I grabbed it out of the air. "What's my challenge, Ronark?"

He eyed me up and down, thinking. Then he threw back a gulp of beer and said, "No splash."

"Are you kidding me?" I complained.

"Hey," he said, spreading his arms wide. "No one said the challenges had to be fair."

"Fine. I've got this."

At least twenty pairs of eyes were watching me. Holding firmly on to the rope, I kicked off the rock. As I reached the peak of my swing, I pulled my legs upward and aimed my head toward the water. Mid-jump, I shifted into a raven. Cool water rushed over my beak, then my feathers. I spread my wings out under water, and for a moment, it felt like I was flying again. I quickly shifted back to human form and kicked my feet. My head broke the surface of the water, and I took a deep breath.

All around me came a chorus of *oohs* and *ahs*.

"Did that count?" someone in the water asked.

"It totally counted," someone else replied.

"Is that allowed?" another person responded.

I looked up to Ronark on the rock, beaming at him. It sounded like I'd completed the challenge.

He sighed, but there was a smile on his face. "I'll give it to her."

A few girls in the water cheered for me.

"What's my challenge, Jenna?" Ronark asked.

She crossed her arms and smirked. "You know."

He dropped his shoulders. "Seriously? Again?"

"If you didn't want to do it, why'd you stand in front of me in line?" she challenged.

Ronark rolled his eyes and handed her his beer. "Fine. Hold my beer."

"Famous last words," she teased.

Ronark sighed and reached for the waistband of his swim trunks. Before I could look away, his trunks had fallen to his ankles and his package was out there in the open for everyone to see. He was seriously blessed in that department. People all around us whistled and hollered.

"Ronark the Magnificent, everyone!" Jenna announced, gesturing to him like he was a trophy prize.

"Yeah, yeah," he said sarcastically, flipping her off. Then he sprinted to the edge of the rock, jumped to grab the rope, and flipped into the water. He broke the surface a second later, while people continued to cheer. After pushing wet hair out of his eyes, he held up two middle fingers to everyone. "You all can go screw yourselves!"

"With that image in my mind?" the guy closest to him joked. "No way!"

Ronark started swimming toward him, and the guy quickly made a beeline for the edge of the rock, where there was a slope leading back up to the top.

"Ew!" he cried. "Keep your dick away from me, man."

Ronark climbed out of the water and started chasing after him. His bare butt was on full display. I couldn't help but laugh. Even in the midst of everything that these people had gone through, they found a way to make the most of a bad situation.

Jenna took a swig of Ronark's beer, then jumped for the rope and did a flip into the water. Once she broke the surface, she made her way over to where I was treading water.

"Having fun?" she asked.

"It's the most fun I've had all week," I replied, stating the obvious. The last time I'd gone swimming was at Genevieve's lake house. The thought instantly made me think of Venn, and my heart sank. I missed him so much. I wished he was here right now—or rather, that I was with him.

"You okay?" Jenna asked.

I nodded to reassure her. "Yeah, I just miss my boyfriend."

"Aww," she said genuinely, like it was sweet. "Come on. We have work to do."

"Work?" I asked.

"I didn't drag you out here just to catch a glimpse of Ronark's manhood."

"Oh, but it was a fun show," I joked.

"I know." She smiled mischievously before leading me back to dry land.

Ronark returned from out of the trees, snatched up his swim trunks, and slipped them on. A guy in the water groaned in jest.

"Show's over, Brad," Ronark snapped playfully.

A few girls laughed and splashed Brad. He quickly retaliated.

Ronark grabbed his beer from off the rock and downed the rest of it, then made his way over to Jenna and me. "You drank my beer," he accused her.

She shrugged. "You put it in my hand."

"I should've known better," he admitted. "I'm going to grab another one."

"When you're done, we need to talk," Jenna said.

"Ooh," a guy sang as he passed by. "*Someone's* in the doghouse."

"Shut up!" Ronark snapped back. "It's not like that. You want one, Rae?"

"Nah, I'm good," I replied.

"Jenna?" Ronark asked on his way to the cooler.

She shrugged. "Might as well."

Ronark returned and handed Jenna a beer. She cocked her head, and we followed her into the woods. We walked until we were far enough away from the swimming hole that we could hardly hear the hoots and hollers anymore. Jenna sat on a fallen log and took a sip of beer. I sat beside her, while Ronark leaned against a tree.

"What's up?" he asked casually.

Jenna got straight to the point. "We need your help."

His eyebrows shot up. "I'm intrigued. Go on."

"Out of everyone on this island, you've been here the longest. You know Valkas best. If we wanted to..." Jenna exchanged a quick glance with me. I didn't like where this was going. "If we wanted to steal something valuable from him, you'd know where to find it."

Ronark smirked and nodded. "You girls are entering dangerous territory."

"He's right, Jenna," I said. "I don't know about this."

She kept her eyes on Ronark, ignoring my statement. "If it works, we all go free."

His face lit up, but it quickly reverted to normal. "Nobody goes free on this island, sweet cheeks. There's only one way off, and it ain't pretty."

"Unless you happened to have access to the one thing that could kill Valkas," she replied.

Ronark pressed his lips together, looking skeptical. "And what might that be?"

I could tell he didn't believe her. As far as anyone else knew, Valkas couldn't be killed. Jenna glanced to me. Even though I could tell she trusted Ronark, she was deliberately vague.

"That's for us to know and you to find out," she said.

Ronark laughed and tipped his bottle to his lips.

"It's true," Jenna snapped.

He went completely still and slowly lowered the bottle. "You can really kill him?"

She nodded. "He has a dagger that can be used to stop him. Do you know what he would've done with it? Hidden it? Destroyed it?"

"Destroyed it, maybe…" Ronark said in thought. He began pacing back and forth in front of us. "But how do you destroy a dagger? You could break it, but the shards could still kill you. Or melt it down, but where would he find the means on this island? Besides, if it's infused with magic, it might not be able to be destroyed. He might send it off the island, but… no, I think I know exactly what he'd do with it."

He stopped pacing and turned to look at us, a bright expression on his face.

"Well…?" Jenna pressed.

"It's not going to be easy to get," Ronark said. "Nearly impossible, even."

It was like he could read my mind.

"Just tell us," Jenna insisted.

He sighed. "He's got it on him."

"Of course," I muttered.

It sounded so much like him. *Keep your friends close but your enemies closer* kind of thing. Valkas wouldn't trust that weapon anywhere else but where he could keep a constant eye on it.

I turned to Jenna. "Look, this party was fun, but that's it. At some point, I have to accept that I'm a blood slave now and I'm never going to see my friends again. This plan is never going to work."

"You don't know that," she countered. "The least we can do is try."

"Our odds are next to none," I pointed out.

"I thought the same thing about seeing you again, Rachel. I never thought I would." Jenna's eyes pleaded with me.

"Yeah, but this…" I shook my head.

"What's the worst that could happen?" she argued.

She had a point. I could die trying, but what did that matter? Valkas had to be planning worse for me anyway. Might as well go out with a bang.

"I… I guess it's worth a shot," I admitted. "As long as you realize it probably won't work."

"Don't say that," Jenna insisted sternly. "If Ronark's right, all you have to do is get him alone."

I pressed my lips together in thought. "I guess that's pretty easy if he decides to feed on me again."

Ronark scoffed. "Not unless you want to get yourself killed. Where do you think he's keeping it? On his belt? In his boot? On a sheath strapped to his thigh? You only get one guess, sweet cheeks—"

"Don't call me that."

"And if you don't guess correctly, it's game over," he concluded.

Jenna glanced between the two of us nervously. Her plan was already starting to crumble. "So, what do we do?"

Ronark turned and gazed off into the forest, taking another sip of beer. "Wait for the end?"

"Oh, don't even with me!" Jenna shot to her feet and stomped over to Ronark. She grabbed him by the shoulder and forced him to turn around and look at her. "You have *not* given up."

"What makes you say that?" he challenged. "I've been here eight years, snatched during my first shift before anyone even knew what shifters were! I never got to finish college. I don't even know what the outside world is like now, except what I've heard from the rest of you. What's there to go back to?"

"Come on, Ronark," Jenna pleaded. "I know you don't truly feel that way."

"Oh, yeah? And how come you think you know me so well?"

Jenna stared him in the eyes and softened her tone. "Because we wouldn't be having this conversation if you thought that. You're always telling me there's more than this."

"Those are just hopes and dreams," he said.

"Exactly," Jenna replied. "You're the one who told me I get to choose how I react. This is it. This is my decision."

Ronark's shoulders fell. "When'd you become the smart one, Collins?"

She smiled. "The day I met you, Eli."

"Oh, come on," he complained. "You know I hate it when you call me that."

"Okay, okay." She held her hand up in surrender. "I'll drop the pet name for good, but you have to help us."

Ronark pressed his lips together. "You two really think you can do this?"

"No." Jenna looked to me. "I *know* we can."

Her confidence in me was astounding.

Slowly, a grin spread across Ronark's face. "Now that's the kind of attitude I'm talking about. But you're going to need at least four or five shifters to take him on."

"Why?" I asked. I couldn't believe we were actually going to go through with this.

Ronark shrugged. "Conservative estimate. He's strong. A good shifter or two might be able to take him on, but you need more than just a distraction. You need to immobilize him."

"So we gather a team and sneak in during the day while everyone's asleep?" I guessed.

"No, no." Ronark quickly shot my idea down. "Too risky. There are guards stationed in every hallway."

I furrowed my brow. "Not the last time I was in there."

"When was that?" Ronark cocked an eyebrow.

"Um… the day of the incident, the one where that guy died."

Ronark scoffed. "You got lucky. Valkas corralled his guards to deal with that security issue. On any given day, you'd run into at least four guards before you hit Valkas's room."

"So we create a distraction," Jenna offered.

"No. I think I might know something that could work better." Ronark sat on the log beside me, and Jenna joined him on his other side. We both leaned in close while he whispered, "Valkas's Awakening Ball is coming up in just under a week."

"Awakening Ball?" I asked.

"It's a celebration he holds every year to honor himself," Ronark explained. "Dumb, really, but the Soulless eat it right up. It's the anniversary of the day he escaped the island."

"How's that going to help us get close to him?" Jenna asked.

"Each year, he puts on this grand march ceremony where

blood slaves carry him into the ballroom on one of those big carriage-like things with the poles. You know what I'm talking about, right?"

Jenna nodded. "It's called a litter."

"Right. I just so happen to know the vampire who coordinates the whole thing." By the way he said it, it sounded like he was her blood slave. "I can make sure we're on that list to carry him in."

Jenna smiled mischievously. "And we strike before he ever makes his grand entrance."

"Bingo," Ronark confirmed.

"Are you sure that's going to work, though?" I questioned. "That he'll actually be alone?"

"Darling, I've been watching these things go down for years. Valkas is so vain he wants everyone to witness his grand entrance. I assure you we can get him alone beforehand."

"What about me?" I asked. "Valkas knows I'm a threat. He's not going to let me alone with him without his witch body-guard present to play puppet on me."

"Good point," Jenna agreed. "And Rachel has to be there. She has to be the one to do it."

Ronark didn't ask why, like he trusted Jenna without question. "We could disguise her..."

"Too obvious," Jenna said.

Ronark turned to me. "Then I guess, princess, you're going to have to find a way into that litter on your own."

I didn't like what he was suggesting. Not one bit. But if I was going along with this, I had to make some sacrifices.

It was time I made my first one.

13

My opportunity came that night when I was summoned to the chateau. Anton came to my cabin to collect me and led me to a fancy dining room I hadn't seen before. There was a long mahogany table set for twelve, with a big chandelier hanging over it and a fireplace beside it. The red drapes had been pulled back so that moonlight spilled through the tall windows.

"You must wear this," Anton said, gesturing to a dress that hung from a sconce on the wall.

I eyed the silky black evening dress and matching high heels. "I'm comfortable in this, thanks."

"No choice. Lord Valkas requires it."

I pressed my lips together. If I wanted to have a civil conversation with Valkas, I might as well do as I'm told.

"Fine," I agreed, "but I'd like some privacy."

Anton nodded and turned out of the dining room, leaving me alone. I glanced toward each of the doors leading out of the room in various directions while I pulled my pants and shirt off and slipped into the dress. It was a perfect fit, but the neckline plunged so far that the girls were practically playing peek-a-boo with each other. At the base of my cleavage was a feathery beaded brooch that I might've liked if it wasn't just there to draw Valkas's nasty eyes.

Just as I was pulling on the shoes, the door farthest from me opened. I kicked my clothes and boots under the decorative table in the corner and straightened.

Valkas entered with a smile on his face. He wore a black suit with a red tie, looking like some sort of stockbroker or something. "Rachel," he greeted, like we were old friends.

"Valkas," I said coolly as my spine stiffened.

He stopped at the head of the table opposite me. "What is it, darling? You don't like the dress? I thought it would suit you quite well."

"It does," I lied. "I just didn't know you knew my name."

He waved his hand nonchalantly. "Darling, nothing stays secret for long on this island. *Especially* from me." He leveled me with a challenging glare that sent a shiver down my spine. "Please, take a seat."

I sat where he gestured at the opposite end of the table from him. The long table was like a football field between us, which I suppose was a good thing, but it also felt highly impersonal.

Valkas sat, then rang a bell that was set next to his glass.

"To what do I owe the pleasure?" I asked, placing my napkin in my lap—only because that felt like the proper thing to do.

Just then, a line of servants came through a swinging door, which I presumed led to the kitchen. *What does a vamp need a kitchen for?* I thought briefly.

The woman in front pushed a cart to my end of the table and set a plate of steaming food in front of me. The scent of garlic, onions, and a mix of spices filled my nose. My mouth watered at the sight of a juicy steak and roasted potatoes. I reached for my fork immediately, but I slowed when I remembered who was serving it to me.

The woman leaned over and filled my glass with water without a word. Across the table, another servant poured a thick red liquid into Valkas's glass. Between us, a different woman threw another log of wood in the fire, then they all turned in unison and headed back to the kitchens.

Valkas took a sip of blood, then smacked his lips before responding to my question. "I just thought we could have a nice dinner together."

"You must forgive my caution," I said flatly.

"Go ahead, Rachel," Valkas insisted. "It's not poisoned. If I wanted to poison you, I would've done it in the dining hall in the slave quarters. Actually, I wouldn't have even waited that long."

That was very true. I lifted my knife and cut into the steak. Its savory flavor filled my taste buds with so much pleasure that I might've stayed on this island just for the food.

"Delicious, isn't it?" Valkas said with a smile. "It will give your blood a nice... *juicy* flavor."

I immediately slowed my chewing and set my knife down. "Is that why you brought me here? To feed on me again?"

"Oh, no." Valkas spoke slowly and took another sip of his drink. "That is merely a perk of the meeting."

"What am I here for?" I suddenly remembered how much Valkas hated questions. He didn't seem to notice this time, though.

"I want to make you a proposition."

I poked a potato with my fork and glanced up at Valkas across the table. The look in his eyes told me he was serious. I contemplated how to phrase my next question without asking directly, *'And what makes you think I'd agree to that?'*

"A girl like me doesn't often negotiate," I said before popping the potato in my mouth.

"That's because a girl like you doesn't know what she wants." A shadow passed across Valkas's silver eyes, making them look even darker.

He was wrong. I knew exactly what I wanted. *Safety.* Safety for my family. For my friends. For the world. And that was never going to happen as long as there were vampires alive. I didn't care what the government thought about their *rights*. Vamps thrived off evil tendencies and didn't care who they hurt in the process.

"What is it that you think I want?" Woops. Another question. Though this time, his eyes brightened, like he was more than happy to answer.

He leaned back in his chair and gestured around himself. "What does *everyone* want, Rachel?"

I went silent, not sure if he actually intended for me to answer.

"Power," he said. "Wealth. There is nothing else."

Maybe to him there wasn't. But to me, there was family. There was happiness. His power couldn't earn him that.

"When you have those two things," he continued, "you don't need anything else."

"But if everyone's powerful, no one is," I countered, taking another bite of potato.

Valkas smirked. "Not everyone gets what they want, darling. Only the best of the best can achieve greatness. Everyone else follows because they think they can experience greatness vicariously through their master."

Bingo! That was exactly how he'd amassed a following of

Soulless. They wanted a piece of the winning pie. I was sure it was the same with Rogers, too.

"So this proposition… it would provide me with power."

"Oh, yes," Valkas replied with a greedy look in his eyes. "More power than you can possibly imagine." He stood and began pacing toward me, slowly running his fingers across the back of each chair as he went. "Can you imagine it, Rachel? A world where we controlled the wealth, where people complied to our every demand, where we were worshiped as gods?"

He stopped behind the chair next to mine and stared down at me with a hungry look in his eyes. I felt like I might puke up my steak.

"You want me to join you," I said without emotion. Right now, it was best if I masked it. I wasn't going to get anywhere by ramming my steak knife through his hand, which I was honestly considering.

Valkas held his head up proudly. "You are a powerful witch, Rachel. With some training, you could be the best."

"And only the best deserves to be at your side." I smiled, playing my part, as if the thought of running the world pleased me.

I didn't have to ask him why he would propose such a thing. *Keep your friends close but your enemies closer* never rang truer than in this moment.

And that's when it hit me. Valkas had been bluffing about trapping my soul. He didn't know how. That, or he didn't have the means. The next best option was getting me on his side, where he could keep a close eye on me. In his eyes, he surely thought he could manipulate me into giving up the fight—as long as the reward was worth it. And if I had all of that, all the power and wealth he'd promised, he might think he had a chance at convincing me to change for him. That way, as an immortal vampire, I'd never come after him again in a reincarnated form.

That was never going to happen, but it just so happened to be the very cover I needed right now.

Valkas stepped behind my chair and brushed the hair from the back of my neck. I shivered beneath his cold touch, but I otherwise remained calm. He bent to whisper in my ear.

"I strive for the best in all areas of life, Rachel. And I always get what I want."

I turned my head to look up at him. "That's a very generous offer."

"Yes, well, I'm a very generous person," he said proudly.

I resisted the urge to snort. "What about my sister?" I couldn't seem too eager to accept his offer. That would only arise suspicion.

Valkas rounded my chair and sat in the chair to my left. "What about her?"

"Correct me if I'm wrong, but I believe this is a negotiation."

He thought about it for a moment before answering. "Yes, I suppose it is."

I almost let a smug smile find its way across my lips. "If I were to go along with this... to join the Soulless... then I have one request."

"Your sister's freedom," Valkas guessed.

"Yes," I answered. "She gets full immunity from any harm. Your men shall not touch her or harm her in any way."

He pressed his lips together in thought. I could tell it was hard for him to accept a negotiation. He liked to be the one in charge. But he also *really* wanted me by his side, where he could keep watch over me for eternity.

"I think that can be arranged," he finally agreed. "I have to say, I thought you'd take more convincing."

I almost panicked, but I shrugged for show. "Like I said, it's a generous proposal. All I want is for my sister to go free. Then I'm more than happy to enjoy the power and wealth you've offered."

Valkas's lips curled into an evil grin. "You're a wise woman, Rachel."

Ha! *Woman.* No one had ever called me *that* before.

"So, you will join me?" he asked.

I took a sip of water. "I thought we already established that."

"I need to hear you say it, darling." Valkas took my hand in his and stood from his chair. Then he lowered himself onto one knee. Definitely not how I pictured my first proposal. "Rachel, will you do the honor of becoming my right-hand woman and helping me conquer this world?"

Pushing down the bile rising to my throat, I answered in the softest, sweetest tone I could muster. "I will."

Valkas pressed his slimy lips to the back of my hand, then flipped it over so it faced palm-up. His fangs elongated.

"Whoa." I pulled back slightly, but not enough to escape his grasp. He held on to my wrist tightly, and it became very apparent why Ronark cautioned me against doing this alone. He was *strong*.

Valkas looked up at me, and darkness crossed his eyes. "I thought it was apparent what would happen next. I must give you the mark of the Soulless to secure our deal."

"Fair enough," I said, though I really, *really* didn't want the mark of the Soulless on my wrist. "I just thought..." I paused for dramatic effect.

"Thought what?" Valkas growled, clearly starting to get annoyed.

"I thought there'd be a big ceremony or something. We could announce this in front of the entire island. It would mark the beginning of a new era for the Soulless."

Valkas paused for a moment. "And when would we do this?"

"Your Awakening Ball, perhaps?" I suggested, holding my breath. If this didn't work, I was going to crap diamonds. All hope would be lost.

Valkas dropped my hand and stood. "You make a fair point. We will announce it in a week's time. That will give me plenty of time to coordinate our first strike in the new war against humanity. And you, my darling, will fight alongside me as my queen."

He pressed his lips to the exposed skin on the side of my neck, his fangs trailing along my skin without breaking it. My breath wavered momentarily. Convincing Valkas I would fight alongside him had been far too easy.

That's when I realized a horrifying truth. There were likely things about Valkas's plan he had yet to reveal to me. He could very well be playing me for an even greater purpose.

I just had to beat him at his own damn game.

14

I was counting down the days until the Awakening Ball. Five days had passed since my meeting with Valkas when Ronark invited Jenna and me into his cabin to discuss the plan.

"Be careful what you say," I warned in a low voice. "I think I'm being watched."

I knew how guys like Valkas worked. He pretended like I was nothing more than the dirt on his shoes, inviting me to fancy dinners with him only to put me on the menu for dessert—and yeah, it had happened more than once this week, and I'd had to stomach it for the sake of our plan—only to toss me back to the slave quarters when he was done with me.

But I think he did it because he thought I was more comfortable in the slave quarters and around my sister than I would be up at the chateau. It was his way of luring me into a false sense of security. But I couldn't shake this feeling—the one that made the little hairs on the back of my neck stand up —that I was being watched. Which didn't surprise me in the slightest. It just meant I had to be cautious.

"We're all shifters here," Ronark said, glancing from my sister to me, then to the shades that were drawn over the window. "They can't hear us."

"Still, keep your voice down," I said. "What kind of shifter are you, anyway?" He looked like he might be something small and gentle, like a hamster or something.

Ronark held up a hand to stop me. "Believe me, sweet cheeks, you don't want to know."

"So, did you get us on the list?" Jenna cut in.

Ronark smirked. "Yep. I've got Andi and Brad on the list, too, and they're all for taking Valkas down. I trust these shifters with my life."

"And me?" I asked. Valkas and I had agreed to make our big announcement during the Awakening Ball, but he never agreed to have me ride in the litter with him. One way or another, I had to get to the staging area, where he'd be alone and it'd be seven against one.

"I'm still working on that, sweet cheeks," Ronark replied. "It's hard to convince my mistress without admitting I know what's going on. I have to make her think it's her idea."

"Or I need to convince Valkas," I said. "He's not the kind of guy who would want to share the spotlight."

"Which is exactly why I think we need a Plan B, C, and D," Ronark said. "We have one shot at getting this guy alone. We can't screw it up."

My stomach twisted. I still wasn't sure this would work.

Just then, voices came from outside, more than I expected to hear this early in the morning. Usually, the slaves came back from the chateau one by one, not in a huge group, and we still had an hour until sunrise. Jenna and Ronark exchanged a quick glance, and they both frowned.

"What?" I asked in alarm. "What's going on?"

Jenna pushed away from the wall where she'd been lean-ing. "New recruits."

I hated the way people used the word *recruits* around here… like they had a choice.

"Come on." Jenna turned toward the door. "We should go help them find their cabin assignments. Tonight's been rough enough for them as it is."

The three of us stepped outside to see a group of fifteen people surrounded by half a dozen vampires. Other blood slaves had emerged from their cabins and were whispering among themselves.

"Jackson," one of the recruits hissed at the guy beside him, elbowing him in the ribs. He looked young, but he had a long brown beard. The guy beside him—Jackson—was the spitting image of him but with a shorter beard. They wore matching plaid shirts and reminded me of lumberjacks. "Shh…"

"You!" one of the closest vamps said, pointing toward the three of us at the cabin door.

My heart jumped a little until Jenna stepped forward.

The vamp handed her a piece of paper. The mark of the Soulless peeked out from under the sleeve of his leather jacket. "Get them to where they need to go. Their initiation begins tonight."

"Yes, sir," Jenna said confidently.

He turned on his heel and started for the trail leading back up to the chateau. The other vamps followed behind him. The new blood slaves huddled together, throwing glances this way and that.

"I know how hard this must be for all of you," Jenna started, but I didn't hear the rest of her speech.

My gaze fell upon one of the faces in the back of the group. The guy's eyes connected with mine, and he looked at me like I was the only girl in the world. All the air whooshed out of my lungs, and my knees went weak beneath me. Time stood still as I tried to make sense of what I was seeing.

Dark skin… tight curly hair… I'd know those brown eyes anywhere. What was he *doing* here? Was I hallucinating or something?

Relief momentarily washed over his features. It was quickly replaced by a glistening in his eyes, like he might burst into tears at the sight of me.

Seeing Venn standing in front of me was like the moment you reach the top of a rollercoaster. You feel your heart lift in your chest, and you hold your breath until you think your lungs might burst. For a moment, everything is quiet and still. Then *Bam!* You reach the edge, and your heart flies up into your throat. Every inch of your body pulses with adrenaline. A moment later, the track levels out, and you realize you were never in any danger at all, but still… you can't tame the pounding of your heart and the quaking of your fingers.

Emotions I couldn't even put names to whipped through me so fast that it left me lightheaded. My whole body lit up in desire for him. It was like I could feel every nerve ending come alive, leaving me shaking and on the verge of tears. All that mattered was running into his arms and holding him again. I'd missed him so much.

I started toward him, prepared to rush into his arms, but Ronark grabbed hold of my wrist and pulled me back. I just about clocked the guy in the jaw, but then I caught the look in his eyes.

He lowered his voice. "You're being watched, remember?" He glanced around like he might spot a sniper somewhere in the trees. "If you recognize one of them, the last thing you want to do is let the vamps know."

Good point. My heart ached as I stood there, staring out into the small crowd at Venn. My knees shook, as if they wanted to make their way over to him despite my commands for them to stay put. Venn's expression was full of pain, sorrow, and relief, but he remained still. I knew he did it for the same reason that I continued to stand at Ronark's side. But I spotted something soft in his eyes—something I'd seen so many times throughout my lives that it spoke to me in a way words couldn't.

I bit down hard on my lower lip to keep my emotions at bay. He was like a magnet drawing me to him, and keeping my distance was literally causing me physical pain.

Jenna helped guide the newcomers to their respective cabins, separating them by numbers like livestock. When I saw that Venn was headed our way to fill the empty bed in Ronark's cabin, I nearly toppled over right then and there. My heart pounded so wildly in my chest that I thought the vamps might be able to hear it from the other side of the island.

"In, you two," Ronark instructed.

I couldn't get into the privacy of the cabin soon enough. As soon as Ronark shut the door behind us, I fell into Venn's arms.

"You're here!" I cried. I stood on my toes and pressed my lips to his before he could get in a word. Heat pooled in my belly, and my heart pummeled against the inside of my chest. My hands roamed all over him—up his arms, over his back, and in his hair. I had to check that he was there in flesh and blood, that he was real. And by the hands of all that were holy, he was.

I gasped when he drew away, trying to catch my breath. Venn gazed down at me as tears rolled down his cheeks. He looked at me like he was staring into the eyes of a deity—like he couldn't believe I was standing there in front of him.

"God, Rae. I missed you so much it nearly broke me." Venn's voice was like a song, a beautiful, wonderful song. He pulled me back into an embrace and buried his face in my hair, inhaling my scent like he craved it more than anything else in the world. We rocked from side to side as he held on to me with such tender loving care. "I was so worried about you."

I let my tears soak into the front of his t-shirt. "I can't believe you're here."

"I can't either," he whispered in my ear, his voice cracking. My spine tingled, but in a good way. "But it's really me. I swear."

"I don't mean to interrupt your... reunion," Ronark said. I'd barely remembered he was there. "So I'm going to go."

I heard the door creek open and then shut, but I didn't take my head off Venn's chest. I just wanted to hold him until the end of time.

"You shouldn't have come," I finally said. "It's dangerous here."

"I know." He drew away from me to look me in the eyes again. Tears stained his cheeks. "That's exactly why I had to come."

Swoon.

"Why?" I whispered. "Now you're stuck on this island with the rest of us."

Venn took a deep breath. "I know. It was reckless and impulsive."

I chuckled, mostly because the emotions tearing through me had left me overwhelmed. "It sounds like some of my personality is rubbing off on you."

Venn smiled. "Yeah, it might be. I just couldn't handle not knowing what had happened to you."

We stood there in silence for several minutes, just wrapped in each other's arms. Finally, I spoke.

"Do you have any plans for getting off the island?" God, I hoped he wasn't as stupid as I was. "Because clearly my plan didn't work."

Venn dropped his gaze. "I'm still working on that."

"Yeah, me too. How'd you get here?" I asked.

He shrugged. "I ran into some trouble along the lakeshore."

"When you say *ran into trouble*, you mean *sought out the Soulless*," I accused lightly.

Venn smirked. "It was the only way to find you. I traveled from bar to bar until I found a guy with the mark on his wrist. I had a little bar fight and… let them take me."

"Venn," I said breathlessly. "You shouldn't have. Did they hurt you?" He looked okay, at least.

He shrugged. "They got a couple of good punches in, but that was almost a week ago already."

"A week? Where have you been all this time?"

"Detained," he answered vaguely. "Until they put us all on a boat and brought us here."

My heart sank. "They don't know who you are yet, do they?"

He shook his head. "No, I don't think so. As far as they know, I'm just some random guy."

I hugged him tighter, even though all I wanted to do was yell at him for being reckless. Then again, I shouldn't exactly be the one to talk. What he did was incredibly noble, and I was glad he was here with me now.

"I'm sorry," I whispered after a brief silence.

Venn ran his fingers through my hair. "Sorry for what?"

"For leaving."

He pressed his lips to the top of my forehead, warming my skin. "I'm just glad I found you."

I wiped the tears from my eyes. "Why did you come?"

Venn's eyes searched mine, like he couldn't tell what I was feeling. "I came for you."

"But… aren't you mad at me?"

His eyebrows knitted together. "Mad?"

I nodded. "For leaving without telling you."

Venn sighed and led me across the cabin to sit on the lower bunk. "Honestly, Rae, I was upset and a little hurt when you left."

I knotted my hands together in my lap. "I'm a terrible girlfriend, aren't I?"

"No," he answered.

"But… we're supposed to be soulmates. And I just… left."

Venn tilted his head in question. "I don't think you understand. Being soulmates isn't an easy way into a relationship. It doesn't mean we'll be perfect. It just means that we have a strong connection. It's what we do with that connection that matters. The connection dies if we don't nurture it."

He wrapped an arm around my shoulder, and I leaned into him, absorbing what he said. I'd never had to work on a relationship before. I'd just assumed they either worked out or they didn't.

"We're a team, Rae," Venn whispered. "Being part of a team takes a lot of work."

I nodded as what he said began to sink in. "I'm glad we're part of the same team."

"Me, too." Venn drew away from me to look me in the eyes.

Slowly, he leaned down until his lips were hovering just

millimeters away from mine. That split second before the kiss, all the anticipation leading up to it, was everything. My breath caught in my chest, and my heart lifted until it felt like my entire body was floating.

Then his lips connected with mine, and I completely forgot I was on Gregor Island, surrounded by hundreds of the most ruthless vampires in the world. All that mattered were Venn's lips on mine and his words echoing in my head. *We're a team, Rae.*

I'd be damned if I let my team fall apart.

For the first time, I was starting to get a sense of what Jenna meant when she said that even when we've given up hope, there was still a chance.

"Venn." I drew away, panting. I pressed my forehead to his and gazed down at our entwined fingers.

"Rae," he whispered back. I loved hearing him say my name.

"Are you scared?" I asked.

"Absolutely." He wasn't even afraid to admit it, and that, I felt, took a level of courage I didn't have. I admired him so much for it. "Every day I was without you, I was terrified."

"Me, too," I whispered, closing my eyes. A knot formed in my chest. It was harder to admit than I thought. "I know I'm the Ravenite and I'm not supposed to be afraid of anything, but I am, Venn. I'm just as scared as everyone else."

"Hey," he said lightly, pulling my chin up. "That's okay. Remember what Sondra said? It's okay to feel fear. It's how you use it that matters. I know you, Rae, and I know you'll use it to fuel your determination."

Determined. Resolute. Hell yeah, I was!

I nodded as the knot in my chest began to loosen, as if his

words had the power to unravel my unease. All the hopelessness I'd been collecting suddenly seemed irrelevant.

In that moment, Genevieve's words came back to me. *You should know that there's always more than one way off an island.*

Did she know this was going to happen? She couldn't have.

But there had to be something to what she said. Jenna had been trying to convince me of it for days. There *was* another way off this island. There *was* a chance to retrieve the dagger again. We could do this. Together.

"I'll use my fear wisely," I promised.

Venn took my face gently in his hands, guiding my gaze to his. "I know you will."

I lifted my chin to brush my lips across his mouth again. It felt so good, like being in his arms was where I was meant to be—like we were meant to face all of this together. I just wished I could show him how much I loved him.

My hands found their way under his shirt, and I ran them up the bare skin on his back. His fingers tangled in my hair, and he pulled me in until I crawled onto his lap. My whole body shook against him. In that moment, it was as if Venn and I were alone in the world—like there weren't any vampires outside our cabin and we weren't facing a war with impossible odds.

Just us, I repeated to myself, feeling as if time had come to a standstill and the statement was irrevocably true.

I tugged at Venn's shirt until he drew away from me just long enough for me to pull the shirt up over his head. A moment later, his lips were on mine again as my hands roamed his body. I lifted my arms and grabbed hold of the top bunk to steady myself. Venn took my shirt off and tossed it onto the floor. Gently, he wrapped his arms around me and lowered me to the bed. I grabbed for the sheets and pulled them down as we both kicked our shoes off.

Venn's hands found the skin above my waistband and began inching their way up my body. His lips left mine to trail down my neck and to my bra strap lying across my collarbone. I gasped as tingles of excitement spread their way across my skin. Heat pooled between my thighs, and my heart pounded so hard I could feel it shaking my entire body.

"Are you sure about this?" Venn whispered against my shoulder.

I'd never been surer about anything in my life. Yeah, most people might've waited until all of this was over, until they were sure they were safe, but for me, safety was a luxury. Somewhere between all the vampire slaying, I had to live my own life… which I hadn't allowed myself to do in years. I might as well start sooner than later.

"Yes," I breathed, pulling him in closer to me and planting a passionate kiss on his lips. "Venn, I love you."

"There's no rush," he said.

I couldn't help but smile. No one had ever treated me with such tender care before. "I know."

"There will be plenty more opportunities when we make it out of here," he continued. "If you're only doing this because you think we won't—"

"I'm not," I assured him. "I *want* to do this. My life is crazy, Venn. That's not slowing down anytime soon."

He smiled.

"Unless you don't want to…" I started.

"Rae," he said like I was being ridiculous. "I've never wanted to be with anyone more than I want to be with you."

Tears pricked at my eyes again. How'd I find such a

wonderful man? My voice came out a mere whisper. "Then be with me."

Venn's lips came down on me again, and I inhaled a sharp breath. Reaching his hand beneath me, he undid my bra and tossed it aside. My chest heaved as his hand roamed over the swell of my breast. I wanted more. So much more.

My fingers trailed down to undo his belt. He kicked his pants off, then unbuttoned mine beneath the sheet. Venn's bare legs were warm against mine, and it only made me want him more. I didn't even know that was possible. My thighs burned for him.

"Please," I begged in his ear.

"Please what?" he asked, teasing me.

I could hardly get the words out past my shallow breaths. "Please. I want to be yours forever."

"You will. I promise."

He sealed the promise with a kiss, then relaxed into me. We gasped in unison. I thought it would hurt, but it didn't. It felt warm and comforting… and *right*.

"Venn," I moaned as he moved against me. Fire raged through my veins.

He pressed his lips to the sensitive skin just below my ear, sending a wave of pleasure down my spine. My breath caught as he pressed into me faster. I squeezed my eyes shut tightly and sank my teeth into his shoulder to keep quiet.

Venn took shallow breaths as his lips roamed over me. His fingers fisted in my hair, and he claimed my lips for his own. His tongue slid inside my mouth, and he kissed me with a passion I'd never felt before. My fingers clawed at his exposed back. He pulled away to kiss my neck, then nipped at my breast.

"Oh my God," I whispered. I couldn't help but let the

words slip out of my lips. Being with Venn was unlike anything I'd ever experienced before. It felt like I'd stumbled upon a magical object capable of harnessing all the pleasure from the world and channeling it into myself. It felt so good I thought my heart might burst into a million tiny little stars. Nothing—and I mean *nothing*—could compare to the way I felt when Venn touched me. His skin on my skin… it was like Synchrony itself had blessed me with all the magic in the world.

Venn's hand moved up my side, to my breast, and then down again, until finally landing between my legs.

"Oh *God!*" I cried into his shoulder as he gently massaged me.

My chest heaved beneath him as that magical force built within me until it burst, sweeping through my body like strong waves crashing into a rocky shore. I barely took a breath before he was thrusting against me in a way that made those waves stronger and fiercer. Holy hell, it made it even better.

Venn fell onto his back beside me, panting. Curling up, I rested my head on his shoulder and snuggled into him.

"Venn?" I asked through shallow breaths.

He wrapped both arms around me. "What?"

"After that, I feel like I can do anything."

15

I woke up several hours later in Venn's arms. I hadn't even realized we'd fallen asleep. I rolled over and scooped my clothes up from the ground and began putting them back on. Venn shifted on the bed beside me. I looked over at him and beamed.

He smiled back. "Hey, beautiful."

"Hey."

He reached for me to drag me back into bed, but I just squeezed his hand and said, "Your roommates probably want to get back in here at some point to sleep."

Venn nearly jumped out of bed at the mention of his roommates.

I chuckled. "How much you wanna bet Ronark took one look at the pile of clothes on the floor and headed straight back outside?"

"My bad," Venn said.

My eyes roamed over him as he pulled his pants back on. Images of what we'd done just this morning flickered through my head, and I couldn't help but smile even wider.

"Ronark?" Venn asked. "Is he that guy from earlier?"

"Yeah," I said. "He's friends with my sister. He's going to help us get out of here."

Venn slipped his t-shirt on and turned to me. "How is she? Your sister?"

"Alive and healthy," I answered, which was all I could ever really ask for. "You saw her last night."

"The one with the short hair?" he asked as he sat down beside me.

"That's her."

"She kind of looks like you," he observed.

I shrugged. "Yeah, well, we *are* related."

He laughed and wrapped an arm around my shoulder. "I'm glad you found her."

I leaned my head against him. "Me, too."

"Should we let my roommates back in now?"

I nodded and stood, then headed to the door. When I swung it open, I found Ronark sitting just outside. He turned to gaze up at me.

"Sorry," I said.

"Nah." Ronark stood and waved a hand like it was nothing. Then he leaned in close to whisper, "I would've done the same thing."

"Uh, thanks. Hey, Venn, do you want to grab something to eat?"

Ronark's eyes went wide. "Wait. That's not what you were doing in there?"

I slugged him in the shoulder. "Shut up."

Venn chuckled from behind me.

"Watch this girl," Ronark said lightheartedly, holding on to his shoulder. "She's one tough cookie."

"Hell yeah, I am. Now get some sleep." I waved to Ronark as Venn and I started down the dirt path.

"Hey," he called. "If you see Brad or Dawson, let them know they can come back."

"Will do," I told him. "Thanks for standing guard."

Ronark gave me a salute, then turned inside his cabin.

"He seems nice," Venn said once we were alone.

"Yeah. I can see why my sister likes him." I quickly changed the subject. "How's everyone else doing? Fiona's all right, isn't she?" I missed her.

"Yeah, last I heard."

I opened the door to the bathhouse, which had a kitchen off one of the rooms where we could grab food whenever we wanted. I lowered my voice in case anyone was inside. "Last you heard? When was that? Have they made any headway on finding Matias or his successor?"

"I'm not sure. Remember, I ran into the Soulless not long after you left. I've had no way to contact everyone."

My shoulders fell. "I hope they're okay."

We entered the kitchen, which was basically a bunch of cupboards and countertops with a hand-pump sink in the corner. There were multiple coolers, but otherwise no stove or refrigerator. I pulled a loaf of bread from the corner and began working on sandwiches.

"It's not pretty, but they keep us fed," I said. "Anyway, it won't be long now before we can make our move. But we should probably wait to discuss specifics."

Venn nodded in agreement, then held his palm up when I handed him the sandwich. "I'm actually not very hungry."

I shoved it toward him. "I don't care. You have to eat. You need your strength."

He eyed the sandwich curiously, then took it. "Strength for what?"

I hated that I had to be the one to break the news. "For your initiation ceremony tonight. They'll test your strength to see which vampire you should belong to."

Venn frowned. "That doesn't sound good."

"No, it isn't. My advice? Knock your opponent out. They'll move on to the next fight if it's not entertaining them."

Venn looked nervous.

"With me, Valkas only wanted a source of entertainment. For you?" That wasn't something I wanted to think about.

"For me?" he pressed.

"For you, it's going to be an actual test. And you have to make sure you pass."

***

Venn will be fine. He's a wolf shifter. He can handle anything.

And I meant it.

As night fell, blood slaves began making their way up to the chateau, and the "recruits" were rounded up. I didn't know if I was invited to watch, but I figured no one would notice a cleaning maid missing from the chateau on a night like this.

In the light of the moon, I followed the trail toward the fight ring I'd been thrown into my first night here. Several couples—vampires and their slaves—walked ahead of me on the trail. As they took their seats in the stands, I slipped around the back of the bleachers and stood in the shadows. The hair on the back of my neck stood. It felt like I was doing something wrong, like I wasn't supposed to be here without a vampire to escort me.

Screw that. I wasn't letting Venn face this fight alone.

I watched as more and more couples flooded into the arena and took their seats. My eyes fell upon Jenna as she and her vampire—Silas—emerged from the trees. The sight of him knocked the air out of my chest like a punch to the gut. He was tall, with broad shoulders and thick arms, and he had a scar above his eyebrow.

He was there the night my parents were killed!

Why hadn't Jenna ever mentioned it? She always talked about her vampire so vaguely—when she talked about him at all.

I urged to rush forward and pick a fight with him right then and there. After everything he'd done to Jenna—kidnapped her and forced her to give up her blood for him—he deserved it. But I swallowed down my fury and stayed put. Picking a fight with a vamp on a cliff *full* of vampires wasn't exactly the best idea. I was reckless, but not *that* reckless.

Jenna's expression was unreadable as she followed her vampire into the stands. She acted like a robot. Which I guess was the only way to survive as a blood slave. It was that or show your true feelings and get yourself killed.

Chatter filled the arena, and soon, the chanting took over.

Fight. Fight. Fight.

I knew Venn and the other recruits were picking their weapons right now. I just hoped he picked a good one.

Soon, the entire island was seated in the stands. Valkas walked out of the trees, with Rogers in tow, and the chanting turned to cheers. Valkas held his hands above his head and spun around with a huge smile on his face. He craved the attention, like he was a king. It made me sick.

Sit down already, asshole.

Valkas dropped his hands, and the crowd went quiet. "I

won't bore you with a lousy introduction tonight," he called across the ring. "Let's just have some bloody fun, shall we? Let the games begin!"

The crowd erupted into cheers again. From out of the trees, I saw Anton push a girl into the ring. She stumbled but quickly righted herself before placing an arrow on the bow she'd picked. She'd shoved the second arrow in the back of her jeans pocket.

She whirled around and drew the bow just as a guy twice her size stepped into the light of the torches. He was one of the lumberjack twins, the one with the longer beard, and he'd brought a mace as his weapon of choice.

I was already nervous for her. She was such a petite little thing, and he was huge. If she wasn't a shifter, she didn't stand a chance.

Her arms shook as she anchored the bow to the corner of her lip, then let go of the string. She changed her mind at the last millisecond and pulled the bow to the side just as the arrow went flying off the rest. It interrupted the arrow's trajectory, and the arrow went flying off to the side into the woods.

She realized what she'd done a second later, and her eyes went wide. Lumberjack lifted his ball and chain and swung it at her. She jumped out of the way just in time for the spiked ball to land in the dirt where she'd been standing.

Her mouth moved, but it was impossible to hear what she said over all the cheering. The look on her face suggested she was pleading with him. A heavy weight settled in my stomach like a bag of rocks. The Soulless didn't care whether they pulled innocent people off the streets or not. They'd make sinners out of them one way or another.

Lumberjack swung his weapon at her again, and she

ducked out of the way, somersaulting until she was on the other side of him. She placed her second arrow on the string, then drew back a second time. I held my breath for her.

She let go of the string just as the ball connected with her head. Everything happened so fast that it was hard to process it all. The girl fell to the side the same time the arrow struck the guy in the shoulder. Blood began pouring out of his wound and onto his white t-shirt.

While he was momentarily distracted by the pain, the girl shot to her feet again.

Definitely a shifter, I concluded. There was no other way she could've survived that blow.

Using her bow, she swung it at Lumberjack's head. It connected with such a hard *thwack* that I heard it above the cheers. The crowd screamed even louder at that. The guy stumbled backward, disoriented, and landed on his elbows.

The girl rushed forward to grab the weapon that had flown from his hands. She swung it high above her head, then brought it down straight on his face. I flinched and turned my face away from the scene, but I wasn't fast enough. The image of blood squirting everywhere would forever be seared in my memory.

The crowd went wild. I slowly peeled my eyes back open to see that vampires were on their feet now, cheering for the shifter girl's victory. Meanwhile, she stood in the center of the ring, staring down at the man's mangled features. Her whole body shook.

Valkas stood and made his way over to her. The crowd didn't quiet long enough for him to announce her as champion, but he clapped her on the back and whispered something in her ear. Whatever he'd said didn't seem to soothe her as her shaking legs carried her back toward Anton at the entrance to the trail.

Valkas whirled back around and took his seat on his throne again, then said something to Rogers. Rogers mumbled an incantation, then Lumberjack's body lifted from the ground as if it were attached to strings. Rogers guided it over to a group of vamps in the front row, who all were happy to drape the body across themselves and dig in like it was a Thanksgiving smorgasbord.

What the hell was wrong with them? Couldn't they at least show some respect?

Of course not. They were vampires.

Moments later, another figure stepped out of the trees and into the ring. He was as big as the last guy with the same look and muscular build. It was the second lumberjack twin, the one named Jackson. His eyebrows were tight, and his lips pressed together in a thin line. His eyes fell upon his brother, and I noticed his grip tightened on his sword.

He'd just watched his brother die, and they wanted to see how he'd handle it. I was beyond disgusted.

Jackson glanced around frantically, as if calculating how he might be able to escape. Before he could take in his surroundings, Anton grabbed another recruit and threw him into the ring. My stomach sank when I saw it was Venn. I didn't want him fighting anyone, let alone a guy who wasn't even in the same weight class.

Venn took a defensive stance, holding a dagger out like he was ready to strike if Jackson came too close.

I didn't know if I could watch this. What if the strategy to knock his opponent out backfired? What if Jackson gained the upper hand? Sure, Venn had killed vampires before, but never another human being. I didn't think he'd do it just to save himself.

Survive, Venn. That's all I ask.

I held my breath as the fight began. Jackson swung his sword out, aiming it straight for the side of Venn's neck like he was going to decapitate him. Venn ducked out of the way and jabbed his dagger toward Jackson's arm, where it would do the least damage. It barely nicked him, just enough that I could see a spot of blood, but not enough that Jackson reacted. Jackson spun toward Venn, looking like he was about to shoot fire out of his nose.

Come on, Venn. You can do this.

Jackson took another swing at him, this time at his legs. Venn jumped, just barely making it over the top of the blade. Jackson quickly tried another method. He jabbed the sword toward him like he was going to impale him. I flinched, but when I opened my eyes, Venn had dodged out of the way and spun toward the guy. He grabbed on to Jackson's wrist and yanked him forward, then sliced his dagger across the back of his hand.

The crowd cheered, and Jackson dropped his sword. Venn quickly bent to retrieve it, then tossed both weapons toward the edge of the cliff. The dagger flew into the darkness, while the sword teetered on the edge, then slipped off into the water.

Jackson's eyes went wide as he realized his weapon had vanished. Venn didn't waste any time. He immediately threw a punch at the guy's jaw. He stumbled backward a bit, and Venn took aim again. Jackson regained his composure a moment later and lunged for Venn.

I gasped when Venn slammed into the ground, over two-hundred pounds of muscle squashing him. Jackson drew back his fist and shoved his other hand into the collar of Venn's shirt. He hesitated, then his eyes flickered to his dead brother's body. A moment later, his fist pummeled Venn's face.

My hands shot over my mouth, and my knees shook beneath me.

No! My mind screamed. *Fight back, Venn! I need you. You have to survive.*

I wanted to rush in and help him, but I knew the vampires wouldn't allow it. I'd die right there with him.

That's how it should be, I thought.

My feet moved beneath me before I gave them the command. I was just about to run into the ring, but I stopped myself when I saw Venn's face morph into a black wolf's. Half the crowd shot to their feet in excitement. Meanwhile, Jackson paused as he realized he was no longer holding on to Venn's clothes but on to his fur. Venn's powerful jaws snapped at the guy's hand, and a pained scream broke out above the noise of the crowd.

Jackson scurried off of Venn, distancing himself from him. Venn rolled onto his feet and curled his lips back over his teeth, growling at him.

"Venn, don't," I whispered to myself.

Of course, he couldn't hear me. He lunged forward, and his paws slammed into his opponent's chest. I thought for sure he would rip his throat out, but he only stood on top of him, growling. Jackson's eyes darted around the arena—to the vampires on either side, to his brother's body, and finally to Venn's eyes. His lips moved, but I couldn't tell what he said.

Without ceremony, he shoved Venn off of himself, scurried to his feet, and sprinted to the edge of the cliff. The whole crowd gasped, including me, as Jackson hurled himself into the rocky water below.

Several vamps at the edge of the bleachers rushed over to the edge of the cliff and peeked over. They must've liked whatever they saw, because they turned back to the crowd and began cheering.

Venn had gone as still as a statue, staring out into the dark water like he couldn't believe what had just happened. Relief flooded through me. It was horrible, considering Jackson was as good as dead. If the rocks below hadn't killed him, the water would. No way could he swim back to the mainland without drowning, even if he was a shifter with super endurance. But I was so happy Venn was alive.

Valkas hesitated for a moment, then stood and made his way out into the middle of the ring. "Ladies and gentlemen… our second champion of the night!"

At the sound of the crowd cheering, Venn blinked and seemed to come back to reality. His lips curled back over his teeth, like he wasn't at all pleased by the outcome. He looked two seconds away from ripping Valkas's head off, but we all knew how that would go.

Still in wolf form, Venn's shoulders dropped, and he slumped back toward the other recruits in the trees, appearing more worn out than I'd ever seen him before. Looking at him made it feel like someone had punched a hole straight through my gut. I just wanted to hold him and tell him everything would be all right, even if it was a lie.

I quickly abandoned my hideout in the shadows of the bleachers and raced into the forest after him.

16

"Venn!" I cried, rushing through the trees toward him.

I saw his silhouette shift from wolf to human form. He reached out and steadied himself against a nearby tree. I was almost to him when an arm swung out of the darkness and swooped me out of the air.

I instinctively swung my elbow backward, but my assailant ducked out of the way. My elbow met nothing but air.

"Where do you think you're going?" a deep voice asked in my ear. *Anton.*

I relaxed until he set me back on my feet, but he didn't let go of me. I looked up into his silver eyes behind me. "He's the champion of his round, and he needs medical attention. I would hope the vampire he's assigned to would want him in top shape for his first feeding."

Anton finally released his hold on me. Venn's gaze flickered to mine through swollen eyes. Blood dripped from a large gash on his cheek. His eyes pleaded with me, like he thought it was best if I let him be instead of fighting with the vamps.

I turned back to Anton and spoke through gritted teeth. "May I take him back to his quarters?"

Anton glanced between me and the latest fight in the ring. He huffed. "Fine, but do not make it habit, Raven Girl."

"Yes, sir." I rushed over to Venn and draped his arm over my shoulder, helping support him on our way down the trail. He barely let me help him, but he seemed a little disoriented. "That was quite a beating."

Venn blinked a couple of times, as though he was still trying to process it. "It... it all happened so fast."

"How's your face?" I asked. The blood had reached the bottom of his chin now.

Venn shrugged. "He had quite a punch."

"Yeah, I can see that. He might've given you a concussion, too."

Venn shook his head, still looking dazed. "No, I just..." He pressed his fingers to the raw skin on his cheek and came away with blood-soaked fingertips.

"We'll talk about it once we get you to the bathhouse," I said.

Venn didn't say anything the rest of the way there. I led him inside the bathroom and instructed him to get into the tub. I handed him a wash cloth to wipe his face, then took a towel and headed to the kitchen, where I wrapped ice from one of the coolers in it. When I returned to the bathroom, Venn was lying in the tub with his head leaned back and his eyes closed.

"You okay?" I asked.

His eyes sprang open, and he started. "Yeah, I'll be fine. A healing spell might help, though."

I frowned. "My magic isn't working lately."

"Ice is fine, then." He took the ice pack from me while I

turned and lit the lamp in the corner. I rounded the tub and placed the plug in the bottom, then began pumping the water for him.

"What the vampires do to *initiate* their prisoners is horrible," I snarled in disgust.

Venn shivered as cool water rushed over him. "When they told us what we were going to do—that we had to choose a weapon and fight—most of us thought they were joking. I might've too if I didn't already know how ruthless vamps were. I mean, why would they bring us here if they were just going to kill us?"

"It's their form of entertainment around here."

Venn sighed. "I know. I was being rhetorical."

"It's sick, if you ask me."

Venn scoffed. "Yeah, it's sick you if you ask me, too."

Several quiet moments passed. The only sound came from the water rushing out of the tap. I dared to break the silence.

"What did Jackson say to you, right before...?" I couldn't finish my sentence.

Venn slowly pulled the ice away from his face until his eyes met mine. "That's the crazy part. He sacrificed himself so I could win."

"Sacrificed himself?"

"Yeah. He said, '*I won't become a killer for them.*'"

"He didn't want either of you giving up who you are," I whispered. It reminded me of what Jenna had said to me, how she couldn't choose what the Soulless did to her, but she could choose how she reacted to it. Jackson chose not to play their game. "He wasn't willing to sacrifice his character."

Venn nodded solemnly. "I don't know if I could've done it. Killed him, I mean."

I stopped pumping the water and sat on the floor beside

the tub. Reaching out, I took Venn's hand in mine. "I'm so sorry."

After a beat of silence, Venn spoke so softly I barely heard him. "I don't know if I can do it again, Rae."

"Do what?"

"Be a blood slave."

"Venn…" I wished I could find the words to reassure him, but there was nothing I could say to make this better.

"When you've been a blood slave long enough, feeding becomes a drug. That high you get from it… it screws you up, Rae. I've spent a long time trying to heal after what Maliya did to me."

My stomach twisted at the mention of the horrible woman.

"But…" Venn stared at me with such sorrow in his eyes that my heart tore in two. Tears welled in my eyes for him.

"But what?" I squeezed his hand tighter.

"I'm scared I'll forget all it if another vamp feeds on me."

The bathhouse went eerily silent as his words hung in the air. A lump rose to my throat as I thought about him going through all of that again.

"It's not going to happen," I heard myself say.

Venn eyed me curiously, as if to ask what I meant by that.

"Tomorrow night is the Awakening Ball," I reminded him. "If everything goes as planned, there won't be any vampires left to feed on you."

Venn's lips lifted at the corners. "I hope you're right."

"Hey," I teased. "Don't ever underestimate the Ravenite."

Venn chuckled, but it sounded pained. "Never."

17

B reathe in… and out. In… and out.

The night of the Awakening Ball had arrived, and I was practicing deep breathing exercises like Sondra had suggested to me weeks ago. I'd been working on calming myself and preparing for tonight since I woke several hours ago.

I can do this, I told myself. *Tonight, Valkas will die. Tonight, the vampires shall perish with him.*

Unless he's not carrying the dagger, a little voice in the back of my head replied.

And let me tell you, I squashed that little sucker with my mental hammer faster than you can say *screw yourself.*

"I am strong," I whispered to the walls of my cabin. "I am powerful. I believe in myself."

On the exhale, I pictured all the negative energy leaving my body. I slowly peeled my eyes open and held my palm up.

"*Ardet ignis.*" Flames erupted from my palm, shooting a foot into the air. They were gone as soon as they came, but the test proved to me that the meditation exercise was working.

My powers still weren't as strong as usual, but I felt more in tune with Synchrony than I had since I'd arrived on the island.

The cabin door creaked open, and I looked up to see Jenna arriving back from the kitchens carrying a handful of snacks.

"Hey, Jenna Bean," I said, smiling up at her.

"You hungry?" She held out a granola bar.

"Not really," I replied.

She rolled her eyes. "Eat, Rachel. Nightfall is in less than half an hour. You need to keep up your strength."

I took the granola bar from her, but I didn't open it. Instead, my eyes roamed her features—the angle of her dark bangs across her face, the shape of her straight nose, the paleness of her cheeks. For so many months, I'd dreamed about what it'd be like to see her again. Nothing had gone like I'd hoped, but I was still glad she was here with me right now.

Jenna furrowed her brow, like I was creeping her out. "What?"

"Nothing." I shook my head. "I just can't get over how much I missed you. You're so different than I remember, but the same. You know?"

She smirked and sat beside me on the bed. She wrapped an arm around me and laid her head on mine. My heart warmed beneath her touch. "I know exactly what you mean. You used to be so sweet, and now you... kill vampires for a living."

"Kill first, ask questions later," I teased, stealing Teagan's motto. God, I missed Teagan—and Fiona and the rest of them. I hoped they were figuring things out on their end.

"See?" Jenna teased. "Old Rachel never would've said stuff like that."

"Yeah, well, old Jenna would've laughed more and would've played pranks on her cabin roommates."

Jenna shot me a glance, like she couldn't believe I was bringing that up. "This isn't summer camp, Rachel. Are you saying I'm too serious for you now?"

"No, just more… grown up, I guess."

Jenna snorted. "I'm not *grown up*, Rachel. I'm… I don't know the word for it."

I wrapped my arms around her. "Strong, Jenna. The word you're looking for is *strong*. You've been through so much here, and you've learned how to deal with it."

"Yeah, because I had to in order to survive."

I drew away to look her in the eyes. "Don't downplay this. You deserve credit for everything you've been through. Everyone on this island does. After tonight, it will all be over and you're going to get the chance to take your strength out into the world and make a difference."

Jenna's eyes brimmed with tears. For a moment, I saw a glimpse of the sensitive sister I used to know. "No one has ever called me strong before."

"They didn't have to. Because you already know it's true."

She smiled, but I could tell she was holding back.

"You don't have to be afraid to show your emotions, Jenna Bean," I assured her. "It doesn't make you weak."

She pulled me into a hug so hard it knocked the wind out of me. Her voice cracked when she spoke. "I know. It's just been so long since I've been around someone I felt I could share my emotions with."

I rubbed her back. "Well, I'm here. Always, from now on."

Jenna pulled away from me and wiped her eyes. "It's just about time for me to head up to the chateau."

"Me, too. Valkas wants me *dressed like a queen*, he said." I rolled my eyes.

She chuckled. "Do me a favor, will you?"

"Anything," I promised.

Jenna sniffled. "Make me proud tonight."

I nodded. "I will."

"You look gorgeous," Bri raved.

I turned to the mirror in the private suite I'd been assigned to get ready for the ball. Bri had been waiting there with an endless supply of makeup and a black dress that had more feathers on it than fabric. Apparently, Valkas had personally assigned her to help transform me for the ball.

I gasped when I saw my reflection. I didn't look gorgeous. I looked like a freaking monster.

My eyes were rimmed in dark black makeup, and my lips were a dark shade of red I'd never worn before. Bri had twisted my hair up into an elegant bun, which was the only good thing about the whole ensemble. The dress would've been okay if it weren't for the fact that it was so poofy I could hardly move in it. It had a corset top with lacey straps and beautiful beading I actually liked, but then there were the feathers... so many feathers. They completely covered the skirt and trailed up my back, ending just below where my wings might be if I could semi-shift.

Valkas was mocking me. *You're a raven, but you're my raven. And as long as you're mine, you will never fly.*

Maybe I was looking into it too much, but that was the kind of message I was getting.

I fingered the corset. "Do you think it's a little... much?"

Bri stood behind me and smiled at my reflection in the mirror. "Not at all. Valkas is a very flashy person. I hope I did enough."

"Oh, I think it's enough," I said before turning to her. "He didn't happen to say anything about how tonight would run, did he? He never clarified for me when I'm to arrive at the ball."

Bri started cleaning up the makeup spread out across the vanity. "No, sorry. He didn't say anything to me. I'm just here to make you pretty."

"Thanks."

"No problem," Bri said kindly. "Now if you'll excuse me, I need to get ready myself. My master is waiting."

Bri exited the room, but I caught the door before it swung shut and poked my head into the hall. Two guards stood on either side of my doorway, staring ahead like Secret Service agents.

I cleared my throat, and the guy to my right glanced over at me. He was super tall and all muscle. The other guy was short and stocky.

"Excuse me, but do you know how I'm to arrive at the ball? When can I leave to go down there?" I tried to sound as innocent and curious as I could.

"Don't worry," Muscles said in a gruff voice. "We'll escort you there ourselves."

"I was kinda hoping to arrive in time to see Valkas make his big entrance," I said. "I heard it's really amazing. I would hate to miss it."

The guards exchanged a look at each other, as if I made a good point.

"So, will I be arriving before him?" I pressed.

"No," the first guard said. "You're not to make your entrance until Valkas announces you."

"That's fine. Whatever he thinks is best. Thank you." I

retreated inside the room and shut the door behind me. That act was so totally *not* me that it was embarrassing.

I paced around the room, thinking about what the guard had said. I knew how to get to the staging area and when I was supposed to arrive—Ronark had briefed me on that much —but he'd left the *how* up to me. How was I going to get past the guards unseen? My eyes fell upon a statuette of an angel on the nightstand.

Ironic, I thought. A symbol of purity in the middle of a vampire nest.

My fingers trailed over the outstretched wings. They came to a sharp point, and I decided it was as good a weapon as any. I turned to the bed and took the corner of the sheet between my hands, then tugged as hard as I could. A long piece of fabric tore off, and I used it to secure the statuette to my thigh. The dress was thick enough that it hid the weapon nicely.

I smiled. For the first time in… forever, I was actually going into something with a plan.

A knock came at the door, and Muscles stuck his head inside the room. "Time to go, love."

I held my head high and stepped toward him confidently. Neither me nor the guards spoke as they led me down the hall and to the grand staircase. The chateau halls were dead silent until we reached a wide hallway that ended at a pair of double doors. Chatter, music, and the sound of clinking glasses spilled out into the hall.

From this distance, I could barely see into the ballroom. It was beautiful, with a high ceiling and velvety gold curtains hanging from the tall windows. Everything glittered, from the flames burning in the chandeliers high above everyone's heads to the champagne in everyone's glasses. Most of the vampires were dressed in black, but their blood slaves were in all different colors. Some wore long silky evening gowns, while other were in big ballgowns like mine. I searched the ballroom for signs of Venn, but I didn't see him.

Damn it! He was supposed to meet me out here.

The guards stopped me at the end of the hall so we wouldn't be seen. We stood there in silence. Each passing second, I became more and more worried for Venn. I didn't have the time to wait for him. Where was he?

Maybe he'd been assigned to a mistress and couldn't get away from her. *Yeah, that sounds about right,* I told myself, though I wasn't entirely convinced.

After several minutes of watching the doors with no sign of Venn, I decided that I was going to have to go along without him. We only got one shot to get Valkas alone, and I couldn't miss it—Venn or not.

"It's too bad you don't get to see Valkas's grand entrance," I said to the guards, like I actually cared.

"Nothing we haven't seen before, love," the guard on my right said.

And it won't be something you'll ever see again.

"Would it be okay if I went to the bathroom beforehand?" I asked sweetly. "There wasn't a bathroom in my room, and well… I'm still human."

The guards exchanged a glance.

"Can't you hold it?" Short and Stocky asked.

I gave a fake grimace. "No, not really."

Muscles looked nervous, like the very thought of human bodily functions made him uncomfortable.

"There has to be a bathroom around here somewhere." I turned and started down the hall in the opposite direction, gazing around curiously.

The guards hurried up behind me, like I'd hoped. "Ma'am, you are not permitted—"

"I just don't want to interrupt the ceremony, you know?" I said. "Best to deal with this now." I turned down a narrow, isolated hallway.

"Hey!" Muscles grabbed my hand and spun me around. "You're not to go wandering off."

"Oh, I'm sorry," I said innocently. "I just thought… no, it's okay." I waved my hand like it was no big deal. "I'll hold it. Can I fix my shoe first, though?"

I leaned down to lift the skirt of my dress, and that's when I struck. I slipped the angel statuette from its makeshift sheath and swung it at Muscles. He realized what was happening and ducked out of the way. Staying alert, I saw that the second guard was already lunging for me. I aimed the statuette at the center of his forehead, and it connected with a sick *crack*. The angel's head snapped off and went flying. Short and Stocky stumbled sideways.

Meanwhile, Muscles reached out and grabbed hold of my dress. I yanked away from him, and a satisfying tearing sound filled the hallway. A weight fell from my hips as the top layers of fabric dropped away. I ripped off the last few remaining threads, leaving behind only the thin bottom layer. I suddenly felt like I could move again.

I quickly swung my leg up. The heel of my shoe connected with Short and Stocky's face. Muscles jumped me from behind, wrapping his arm around my neck so tightly I couldn't breathe. Gripping the statuette firmly in my hand, I swung it backward into his face. He cried out, and I spun around to see the angel's wing was poking into his eyeball.

Woops.

The second guard was already on top of me, tackling me

to the ground. He might've been shorter than Muscles, but his biceps were thick, and the guy was strong. So I took to playing dirty. I shoved my fingers in his hair and pulled as hard as I possibly could. I felt the strands disconnect from his scalp as he let out a cry of pain. It was enough to distract him so that I could punch him in the throat. He rolled off of me.

Beside him, Muscles had pulled the angel statuette from his eye. His face contorted in fury, and his growl echoed down the hall as he came at me.

I ducked just in time for him to stumble into one of the wooden benches that lined many of the chateau hallways. It crumbled beneath his weight.

I glanced behind me. Any moment now, someone from the ball would rush out here to see what all the racket was about. Thinking quickly, I reached for one of the broken bench legs.

The guard rolled over and looked at me with his one eye just in time to see the shattered piece of wood headed toward his heart. That was the last thing he saw before his body withered away into a pile of ash.

Short and Stocky lunged for me again. "Bitch," he snarled in my ear as his hands clamped around my throat.

My throat felt like it was on fire as I gasped for breath. The broken pieces of bench dug into my skin beneath me. But in his rage, the guard hadn't realized I still held my weapon in my hand. Smirking, I shoved the stake straight into his heart.

Ash rained down on me, and I sprang to my feet. The hallway was a total disaster, but I didn't have the luxury of cleaning it up. Footsteps were approaching.

I had to get out of there. *Fast.*

I turned in the opposite direction of the ballroom and sprinted down the hall. I rounded a corner at the end and hid in the shadows as I peeked back to see who had come for me. At least six vampires had stopped in front of the scene.

I noticed Rogers there, too. He looked calm and collected, like he wasn't at all surprised by this turn of events—as if he expected such a thing from me. He lifted his gaze and glanced around, but I snuck into the shadows before he saw me.

I hoped.

I hurried down a dark hall lit only by the occasional sconce. Breathing deeply, I tried to picture in my mind Ronark's map he'd drawn me in the sand a few days ago. I was at least two hallways away from where I was supposed to be, but I could make it there without turning back the way I came.

Watch out, Valkas. I'm coming for you.

18

My heart hammered as I raced down the hall. At the end, I found myself in a wider hallway with more sconces lighting up the path. I glanced both ways and saw a long stretch of marble floor that met up with the grand staircase. I hurried toward the main foyer, but the sound of a deep voice stopped me in my tracks.

"Walk faster!" Valkas barked. "I can't believe how incompetent you are."

Shit. I was late.

Valkas came into view. Four shifters walked into the foyer toward the ballroom, carrying the poles of the litter on their shoulders. It looked like a small carriage without wheels. There was the main box with a bench where Valkas sat, with four tall pillars rising toward the ceiling like a canopy bed. Long red curtains draped over the top and wound around the supports. The poles the shifters carried stuck out from each corner parallel to the floor.

Valkas wore a pointed crown and a fur-lined cape. He stared down at the shifters in front of him like they were nothing more than slave animals meant to take care of a king.

"Immortality doesn't make me any more patient," Valkas complained. "Sometimes I swear it's a goddamned curse."

Ronark shot Jenna a nervous glance. *Yeah, yeah, I got it. Where is that Rachel bitch?*

"You know," I blurted. "I can help end that curse."

Valkas whirled around, and his expression shifted. His eyes burned with more rage than I thought one person could hold, and his upper lip curled back over his teeth to display his long, sharp fangs. Four other pairs of eyes turned to look at me, and relief flooded their faces. The shifters took my presence as their signal. They dropped the litter to the ground and sprang on Valkas all at once.

He leapt upward and grabbed hold of the litter supports above him, swinging out of reach of the shifters aimed for him.

Ronark shifted mid-air. He was large, nothing like the hamster I'd been envisioning. He had blond fur and a thick mane, with strong, powerful jaws he snapped at Valkas.

A lion.

Valkas kicked the heel of his foot into Ronark's nose, then dropped back into the litter to knock Andi's and Brad's heads together. Jenna reached up and wrapped her fingers in Valkas's hair the same time Andi shifted into a black jaguar and sank her teeth into Valkas's ankle. Jenna yanked his head backward, and he let out a rage-filled scream. It didn't sound like one of pain, more like of warning.

Brad rubbed his head, like he was a little disoriented, but quickly blinked the world back into focus. He shifted, and his body grew to over three times its normal size. Huge antlers unlike any I'd ever seen before sprouted out of his head.

An elk.

I reached Valkas just as his foot swung out to connect with the side of Andi's face. His crown slipped off his head and into Jenna's hands. My body slammed into his, knocking him out of the litter and onto the marble floor. Before he could right himself, I shifted into raven form and snapped my head toward his face. My beak connected with bone, and I tasted the salt from his skin in my mouth. He screamed again, this time in pain.

Damn it. That was satisfying.

But I didn't get to peck him again before his hands were on me. He pulled me off of him, and I saw that my beak had left behind a deep gash just above his nose.

"You think I'm that stupid, darling?" he drawled. "I knew you'd come for me eventually."

Ronark lunged for Valkas in lion form, but Valkas shot to his feet and threw his hand out. He shoved his fingers into Ronark's mouth and pulled upward, forcing his jaw open. To my horror, he shoved my body straight into Ronark's open mouth.

Panic sent my heart pummeling against my rib cage. The first thing that crossed my mind was to not hurt Ronark. I tilted my head backward and tried to keep my beak from skidding along his tongue. Complete darkness enveloped me, and I couldn't breathe. When I tried, no air filled my lungs, only the smell of cat breath.

Jesus, Ronark. Do you ever brush your teeth?

Speaking of teeth, the sharp bastards were digging into my skin. Ronark coughed, and I went shooting out of his mouth. I spread my wings to slow my momentum, but I still slammed into the wall like I'd been hit by a truck.

Ronark was already on the move, joining Brad and Andi to

help drag Valkas down. But Valkas wouldn't be knocked down again without a fight. Somehow, against a jaguar, lion, and giant deer, he remained on his feet. Jenna had frozen up, still clutching the crown and staring straight ahead.

Valkas became so enraged that color began to fill his face, which I didn't even know was possible with vampires. His eyebrows came so close together that they nearly touched, and he bared his teeth and hissed. All at once, he stopped clawing at Andi's fur and reached out to wrap his fingers around Brad's antlers. He twisted, and the sickening crunch of breaking bone filled the foyer.

Brad slumped to the ground, and his body shrank back into human form. His neck was twisted at an odd angle, and his eyes stared lifeless up at the ornate ceiling. Valkas stared down at him with a satisfied smile as he grabbed hold of Andi's jaws and yanked as hard as he could. He swung her around and let the momentum take her. Her body slammed into the bannister of the grand staircase so hard that the wooden rungs crumbled.

At the same time, Valkas kicked Ronark in the gut with so much force he went flying toward the second level. He bounced off the railing at the top of the stairs and went limp as his body plummeted back toward the hard marble floor below.

It all happened so fast that I'd barely taken a breath before Brad lay dead in front of me and the other two struggled to their feet in pain. My blood boiled as I shifted back into human form. My dress shifted with me, but my hair hung in loose waves around my shoulders since the pins had fallen out.

I threw myself at Valkas. He didn't even stumble as I jumped, wrapped my legs around him, and pummeled his face like my own personal punching bag. His elongated fangs cut into my skin, but I didn't care. Hearing the sound of his nose crunch beneath my fist was so satisfying.

Ronark righted himself and jumped Valkas from behind, digging his sharp claws into his back. Valkas merely swung his elbow backward. It connected with Ronark's face, shooting him off Valkas's back. Meanwhile, Andi had gone for his ankles again, but he kicked her aside like she was nothing more than a kitten playing with his toes.

"Screw you, you son of a bitch!" I cried as my fist raced toward his face again.

But it never made it. His hand shot up to block me, and he grabbed hold of my wrist so hard that I thought he might crush bone. He twisted, and my scream echoed off the walls of the foyer.

Valkas grabbed my ass and shoved me up against the wall, pressing his hips into me. His wild eyes roamed my face, and he inhaled my scent. I used my free hand to claw at his face, but he grabbed that one too and held it above my head. When I dropped my legs from around his waist, I just hung there, gasping for breath as his chest pressed against mine.

"So feisty," he said in amusement. "Just the way I like it, darling. You would've made *such* a nice queen if you'd meant anything you said."

"I suppose you didn't either." I caught Jenna's eyes for a moment, and I knew I had to keep him talking.

Valkas shot me that evil smirk he was so famous for. "Of course not, my dear. I always planned to change you myself. I'll let you rot away in my dungeons. Without blood to sustain you, you'll be as good as dead, but death will always be just out of reach."

The thought twisted my guts. No doubt he'd make sure I

couldn't kill myself, either. Unless I ripped the bars off my cell and sent them through my own heart, there'd be no escape. But I'd have to be strong enough to do that first, and I didn't think Valkas would allow me to become that strong.

He leaned in close, sending his cold breath to rush across the corner of my jaw. "I did plan on waiting until we were in the ballroom, to make a spectacle out of it. So symbolic. The anniversary of the night I escaped this island would be the same night I escaped my one and only threat. It's the only reason I've kept you alive this long. But I'm done waiting. Let's get this over with."

His lips connected with mine, as if he owned me, as if he wanted me in *that* way. His tongue felt like a creature from hell inside my mouth, and he tasted like the dirt at the bottom of a sewage drain.

Suddenly, his body went still. His mouth left mine, and he slumped to the ground, freeing me. I breathed a heavy sigh of relief when I saw Jenna standing there, the point of the crown embedded in Valkas's back.

I spit and wiped my mouth. "Really?" I complained to her. "You couldn't have stabbed him sooner?"

She stared at me with wide eyes. "I-I froze up."

We didn't have time to waste. I dropped to Valkas's side and began patting him down. Jenna quickly joined me in the search for the dagger, while Andi and Ronark ransacked the litter. I pulled off his shoes, and Jenna checked his hips for signs of a sheath. We checked every inch of his body, but it wasn't there. We both looked at each other hopelessly.

I cursed under my breath. "How long will he be out?"

"I don't know," Jenna said in a rush. "Usually when you ram a sharp object through a vampire's heart, they don't bounce back from that."

"Not long, I reckon," Ronark said, wiping blood from his nose and coming up beside us. "He heals faster than the other vamps, too."

"Well, the dagger isn't here!" I cried, patting him down again.

Andi's shoulders dropped, like we were hopeless, and Ronark looked completely confused.

"But I thought—" Ronark started.

The sound of several pairs of footsteps down the hall reached our ears.

"Oh, shit," Jenna said, glancing behind herself. "We have company."

I looked down the hall just in time to see the six vampires from earlier, along with Rogers, sprinting our way. Jenna and I shot to our feet beside Ronark and Andi, ready to take them all on, just the four of us against seven.

But we never got the chance. Rogers pulled a small round glass vial out of his pocket and chucked it into the foyer. It shattered at our feet, sending a puff of red smoke straight up at our faces.

That was the last thing I saw before a putrid scent entered my nostrils and everything went dark.

19

I blinked my eyes open to see thin red fabric draped above my head in a dimly lit room. I blinked rapidly, trying to remember how I'd gotten there. It all came back to me in a rush, and I shot upright in the bed I was lying on.

The sound of someone clicking their tongue came from across the room. I glanced around frantically for signs of my sister, Ronark, or Andi, but I was alone in Valkas's room. I didn't know how long I'd been out, but it felt like less than an hour.

Valkas stepped forward out of the shadows. "Rachel," he said with a frown. "I can't tell you how disappointed I am that you ruined my Awakening Ball."

"Where are my friends?" I demanded. "What did you do to us?"

"The potion?" Valkas asked with a shrug. "Just a little magic to knock you out. It's a complicated little concoction, but it sure comes in handy." An evil grin spread across his face.

"Where are my friends?" I repeated in a calm tone, letting him know he couldn't intimidate me.

Before I could process it, Valkas's lips curled over his teeth, then he jumped forward and landed at the edge of the bed. He pressed his palms to the mattress and loomed over me.

"*What did I tell you about asking questions?*" he spat.

"I want to know where my friends are," I rephrased.

Valkas's hand cracked against the side of my face. "You will show me respect!"

Despite the burning ache across my cheek, I forced my breath to follow a calm, steady rhythm. I couldn't let my impulsive emotions get to me right now. My friends depended on it.

"You should just kill me already," I suggested coolly. "Get it over with."

Valkas straightened his spine and cracked his knuckles. "Kill you? I don't run a charity, darling. Killing you would be an act of mercy."

Yeah, and then I'd just be back for him in my next life.

I chose my next words carefully, trying to draw information out of him. "I don't get what I'm doing here. I thought you wanted to change me."

Valkas smiled proudly. "Oh, I will, darling. But there's something I want to show you first. Something that won't have quite the impact after the change."

Before I could respond, Valkas grabbed me by the wrist and yanked me off the bed. Pain shot through my shoulder, but I bit down my cry.

"On your feet," Valkas snarled, tugging me upward.

I got to my feet as fast as I could and stumbled after him. Valkas moved quickly down the hall, so fast that I had to sprint to keep up with him. I thought we were headed for the main foyer, but instead, he pulled me down another hall and to a door at the end. The door opened to a dark, narrow stairwell. I used my free hand to grab on to the railing to keep from falling down the stairs, while Valkas dragged me by the other wrist.

I didn't know how many stairs we descended, but eventually, we came to a stop at the bottom. The air was cool and damp.

Valkas led me into a long, narrow hall lit by the occasional sconce. Stone walls rose on either side of us, making me feel closed in, like I was walking through a cave. The sound of distant groaning filled the air. I wanted to ask where he was taking me, but I kept my mouth shut.

We reached a T at the end of the hall, and he pulled me to the right. I gasped when I saw what lay on the other side of the wall. A single sconce lit up rows upon rows of bars that ran from the floor to the ceiling. There must've been at least a dozen cells, each one barely large enough for a person to lie down in.

And most of them were filled with people.

"Come," Valkas commanded.

We moved by the cells so quickly that all I saw were shadows inside. I heard gasps from the prisoners, but I couldn't place their voices.

Valkas stopped at the end, the one where the pained groans were coming from. He grabbed the back of my shirt and shoved me forward. I caught myself on the bars and stared into the cell, trying to make sense of the shadow I saw curled up in the corner. A man clutched his stomach, writhing in pain. He wore only jeans. Through the darkness, I could see the long, straight wounds on his back darkened by blood, as though he'd been whipped.

Suddenly, the man threw his head back and let out a piercing shriek. My heart crumbled into a million pieces as the sound of Venn's anguished cry echoed off the walls of the dungeon. It felt as if someone had ripped into my chest, pulled my heart out, and smashed it with a meat tenderizer. I didn't think I'd ever felt so horrified in my life.

I whirled on Valkas. My hands fisted in his shirt, and I shoved him up against the stone wall. "What did you do to him, you bastard!?"

At the sound of my voice, Venn went wild in his cell. He let out a loud *howl* like a wolf and jumped at the bars, shaking them violently. His eyes caught in the light, and I just barely spotted the silver in them before he fell into a ball at the floor of his cell and went silent.

I couldn't feel my limbs as reality struck me like a cold, piercing stab to the gut. Venn was changing. Into a vampire. I didn't want to accept the truth, but it was sitting right there, staring me in the face.

When I finally began to feel my fingers again, I turned my gaze back to Valkas. He wore a proud smirk on his face.

"Do you want to kill me now?" he challenged with a smile. "Now that your boyfriend is a vampire? He won't reincarnate. All vampires are damned."

My hands shook in the collar of his shirt. "You asshole," are the only words I managed to get out.

I wanted to lash out, to punch Valkas in the face and drive a stake through his heart and do whatever I could to show him just how angry and upset I was… but I knew it wouldn't do me any good. There was no way to make Valkas pay for what he'd done.

I stared at Venn lying on the cold floor, shaking. I urged to wrap him in my arms and tell him that everything was going to be all right. But I knew it would be a lie. There was no coming back from vampirism.

My breath wavered as I dropped Valkas's collar and stepped toward Venn's cell. "Venn," I whispered lightly, reaching out for the bars. "Venn, I'm so sorry."

He just lay there, curled in a ball and taking heavy, shallow breaths. It was like he couldn't hear me.

"Venn," I whispered again.

"That's enough," Valkas snarled.

He grabbed the back of my hair, pulling so tightly that I felt several strands pull loose. He yanked my head backward and dragged me away from Venn's cell. It was only when he forced my eyes off Venn that I had a chance to look at the shadows in the other cells. My stomach bottomed out as various familiar faces took shape. What were they all doing here? Was this some sort of sick illusion?

"In you go," Valkas sneered. He swung the door open to the cell beside Venn and shoved me inside.

My palms slapped against the floor. By the time I scurried to my feet, Valkas was already securing the lock on my cell.

"Have fun watching the show." Valkas laughed maniacally as he started back down the row of cells.

As he distanced himself from me, my gaze scanned the dimly-lit dungeons in horror. Across from Venn's cell, Sondra hung from the wall in shackles. Her face was covered in bruises and dry, crusted blood, and her head hung to the side with her eyes closed, unconscious.

In the cell next to hers, a girl with long red hair knelt at the bars of her cell, staring at me with sad eyes. There was dirt caked in Fiona's hair, and her clothes were tattered and torn. Her usually bright eyes looked hollow, and her lips were dry and cracked. Ryland sat on the floor of his cell with his arms crossed, leaning up against the wall and looking furious. Beside him, Teagan paced her cell with her hands balled into fists. They had the same worn look to them as Fiona had, as if they'd been starving down here for days.

I looked to the cell next to mine and saw my sister shooting me a sympathetic expression. Ronark was locked up in the cell beyond hers, and Andi was in the one next to his.

Everyone was here, and it was all my fault.

"You guys—" I started, but Fiona cut me off.

"You don't have to say anything, Rae."

"Bullshit!" Teagan snapped.

A lump rose to my throat. "Tea, I'm sorry."

"Don't call me that," Teagan growled. "I'm so not in the mood."

I glanced to Ryland for explanation, but he just narrowed his eyes at me. It was like he was so mad he couldn't even speak to me.

"Rachel, are you okay?" Jenna reached through the bars between us to take my hand.

I squeezed hers back and glanced to Venn. The sight of him shivering on the floor next to me was unbearable.

"I'm fine," I told her, because it was my go-to response. Honestly, it felt like someone had poured red-hot coals into my chest cavity.

From across the dungeons, Teagan scoffed. She threw her hands up. "Of-freaking-course you are."

"What's that supposed to mean?" I asked, growing irritated. Shouldn't she be happy I wasn't dead by now?

Teagan walked to the end of her cell and gripped the bars, staring daggers my way. "Ryland was right about you."

"Excuse me?" I gaped at her. After everything we'd been through, she was turning on me?

Ryland growled and shot to his feet. "Don't you *dare* talk to her like that. This is all your fault."

"I never meant for any of this to happen," I said honestly. I dropped Jenna's hand and rose to my feet.

"That doesn't matter," Ryland insisted. "*You're* the reason the Soulless came after us. You told them about us and where to find us. We didn't even get *close* to Matias before they captured us and dragged us here."

I felt like I could hardly breathe. "How long have you been down here?"

"A week, maybe," Fiona said calmly.

I gasped. "Have they fed you anything?"

"A little." The way Fiona said it suggested it wasn't much.

"And Sondra?" I asked, gazing toward her unconscious body. "What did they do to her?"

Fiona dropped her gaze. "They beat her so she couldn't use her magic, then put some sort of spell on her to keep her unconscious. She's been like that for days."

I pressed a hand over my mouth as hot tears rose to my eyes.

Fiona looked at me sympathetically. "It's not your fault, Rae."

"How can you still be on her side!?" Teagan yelled at her.

"Ladies, ladies—" Ronark tried to cut in, but Fiona started speaking.

"Because I trust her," she snapped back at Teagan.

"How can you?" Ryland asked, his nostrils flaring. "She was the one who created the vampires. She came here despite the rest of our objections. It's her fault we're in this mess!"

His accusation stung like a slap to the face.

"How can you say that?" I asked in a hurt tone. "I'm here to kill Valkas. I'm here to save everyone."

"Because of the mess *you* made," Ryland pointed out. "If you weren't so damn powerful, the spells you cast in your past lives would've died with you."

"I can't control how powerful I am," I retorted.

"You *can*," Teagan replied. "That's the whole point of magic."

"Then why aren't I so powerful in this life?" I challenged.

"Because you haven't worked on it in this life," Teagan said. "You're too impulsive."

"What's wrong with being impulsive?" I snarled.

"Rachel," Jenna said, as if begging me to calm down.

Ryland cut in. "Look around you!"

At that, Fiona cracked. She shot to her feet and turned on her brother. "We knew the risks going into this! We knew from the start that Rae's sister was her priority. Killing Valkas to stop Matias makes sense!"

"But she *didn't* kill him," Ryland shot back.

"Blaming her for her past lives is bullshit, Ryland!" Fiona continued. "She can't control that any more than you and I can control what *we* might've done in past lives. Who knows what shit we stirred up?"

"Fiona—" Teagan started, but she cut her off.

"Don't try to defend him."

Teagan gaped at her.

Fiona turned back to her brother. "The fact is, neither of you are mad at Rae. You're just looking for someone to blame. You're mad because we couldn't fight off the Soulless when they came for us. Christ, what did you expect? They had us outnumbered five to one! You both need to grow a set of balls and admit that to yourselves instead of turning your anger around on your friends!"

The dungeons went silent for a moment. My skin heated

and my heart raced as a plethora of emotions rose within me all at once. Words couldn't describe how sorry I was for everything that happened to all the people I loved.

"I'm sorry, everyone," I whispered.

"Sure you are," Ryland grumbled.

Fiona, Jenna, and Andi all yelled at him at the same time that I couldn't make out what they'd said. The dungeons went quiet again, and I retreated into a corner of my cell, watching in utter despair as my friends turned on me and Venn transformed into the one monster I despised.

20

Hours passed.

Every now and then, Fiona shot me a sad look. I was so glad to see her, but with Ryland and Teagan angry at me, I never got a chance to speak to her.

Jenna sat beside me in her cell and held my hand through the bars. I sat with my knees curled to my chest and my head dipped low. My mind raced with all the things that went wrong, all the things I should've done differently.

"If I never told Valkas about my family, he never would've found them," I whispered to Jenna, so low that only she could hear me. "If I never came here, they wouldn't have ever been put in danger. Venn never would've come after me and been changed. If I never created Valkas in the first place, vampires wouldn't even exist. The whole world would be a different place, and none of you would be hurt."

"That's not true," she whispered back, but I didn't believe her.

I replayed so many situations through my mind, trying to think back to the one moment where it all went wrong.

Should I have walked away from Venn the first night I met him? Should I have pushed harder to find Jenna sooner? I thought about how I'd come to this island, how I fought Jenna in the ring, when Venn showed up and how happy I was to see him, how much I loved him.

And now I'd lost him. I'd lost Teagan and Ryland, and I was about to lose Sondra, Jenna, and Fiona, too. Even Ronark and Andi would perish in my name. Valkas would make sure of that.

I pressed my face into my knees, making my voice muffled. "After all the time you spent on Gregor Island, I never wanted you to die here."

Jenna rested her head on the bars between us. "Are you giving up?"

"What kind of a question is that?" I asked, raising my head. "There's nothing more we can do."

The only thing we *could* do was wait—wait for Valkas to torture my friends and family in front of me. It had to be the only reason they were still alive. Then wait for him to change me. Wait to rot down here for the rest of eternity…

"Maybe there *is* more," Jenna suggested. "If we put our heads together."

I shook my head as tears rolled down my cheeks. "It's over, Jenna. We tried, and it didn't work—again. We don't get a third chance. We're going to perish down here with Venn."

"No," Jenna insisted with tears in her eyes. "No, I won't accept that."

"Forget it. The Soulless have taken everything from us."

"You're wrong," she countered. "I still have you. I didn't get you back just to lose you again." Tears fell from her eyes when she blinked, dripping down her face and into the fabric of her dress.

"It's inevitable," I argued. "The Soulless have proven time and time again that they're stronger than we are."

I just wanted to spend my last few moments holding her, knowing that the last days of my life were spent in her presence.

"You've been given an opportunity to make this right again, Rugrat."

"How?" my voice cracked. It felt as if a hole had been carved out in my stomach and was only growing bigger each passing second.

"Every moment in your life has led you right here. Do you ever wonder if maybe that's what Synchrony wanted for you?"

I shook my head. "I had my chance, and I failed."

"But what if we got out of here?" she pressed. "Would you give it another shot?"

"There *is* no getting out of here," I argued. "Sondra's knocked out, my magic isn't working, and these bars are too close together for any of us to fit through in shifted form. Besides, don't you think Fiona, Ryland, and Teagan would've tried everything possible by now?"

Jenna lowered her voice, though we were already speaking in hushed whispers. "I have an idea."

My eyes darted to Venn, who lay curled up on the floor of his cell. He'd barely moved since I'd been locked away. My gut twisted in agony.

What about what Valkas said? I questioned myself.

Do you want to kill me now?

If I killed Valkas, I killed Venn. But if I didn't kill Valkas, the rest of my friends would perish. The decision was almost impossible to make. I loved Venn so much, but if what I'd heard about Synchrony was true, his soul was being destroyed right in front of me. What if I never lived another life with him? Was I willing to give him up, not just in this life, but every life to come?

I honestly didn't know.

"Rachel, he's a lost cause," Jenna whispered lowly, but her words cut deep into my heart like a knife.

My chest compressed. "What if there's another way to break the curse?"

Jenna shook her head. "I don't think there is."

"Jenna." My voice cracked. "I don't know if I can do this. If Venn's soul is damned because of me…"

"Rachel," Jenna said softly. "I'm not saying you don't care, because I know you do."

"You're damn right," I said.

"All I'm saying is that when a hard decision comes along, you have to put aside your emotions."

As much as I wanted to retaliate and tell her she was wrong, I couldn't help but think that Jenna had a point.

"Well, that's… a hard pill to swallow," I said. That was the understatement of the year.

Jenna gazed down at our entwined hands. "I want the best for you, Rachel."

A lump rose in my throat as I gazed at my sister's teary eyes. "I can't tell you how sorry I am for everything that happened to you. All I can say is that I'm glad that through it all, you found yourself."

I reached through the bars and pulled Jenna into a hug. It was a little awkward and wasn't the best hug we'd ever shared, but it didn't matter. All that mattered was that my sister was here in my arms.

"Clearly, my big sister still has so much to teach me," I said.

She pulled away and wiped at her eyes. "And you me. I just want to know one thing."

"What's that?"

She took a breath. "Where's the Ravenite you told me about?"

I gaped at her. Was she implying I'd lost everything the Ravenite stood for? *Had* I?

"What happened to all the fight in you?" Jenna asked.

I shrugged. "I guess that's another thing the Soulless took from me."

"No," she insisted. "They can't take that from you unless you let them. I know, because I used to think the same thing. But you can reclaim it, Rach."

"Jenna, you gave me this pep talk days ago, and look how great that turned out. This time, our odds are even worse."

"So you admit we still have odds?" she asked.

I stared at her blankly. I didn't know how to answer. Was I starting to actually believe what she was saying?

"We're going to get out of here, but you have to accept that it may not be on your timeline. One way or another, we'll make it off this island. Together."

"You really think so?" I asked.

Jenna held her pinky finger out to me. "I pinky swear."

I looked down at her finger, unsure if I truly believed her. But the fact was, Jenna had a point. If she felt—in the wake of everything—that there was still a chance, who was I to tell her she was wrong? The least I could do was stand beside her until the moment my soul left my body.

I twisted my finger around hers. "Pinky swear."

"Let's get started," she said before hopping to her feet and raising her voice. "Okay, guys. It's time to put our heads together."

Ryland groaned, but Fiona, Ronark, and Andi all perked up.

"I don't know about the rest of you, but I'm not ready to die down here," Jenna said. "We still have work to do."

Fiona stood. "Whatever it is, I'm in."

"Me, too," Andi said.

Jenna turned to Ryland and Teagan. They exchanged a wary glance.

I pushed myself to my feet and stood at the front of my cell. "I know how hard it must be to trust me after everything I've put you through. I haven't always acted out of everyone's best interests, but I want to make things right. I've always had a rule about death. If I ever end up facing it, I will fight until my last breath. And while my views on death might've changed since meeting you, the principle remains. You don't have to forgive me, but I do ask that we can put our differences aside—at least for tonight—and finish this mission."

"I'm with you," Ronark said.

I turned back to Teagan and Ryland. Teagan dropped her gaze to him, where he still sat on the floor with his arms crossed.

Ryland shot me a skeptical expression. "We've spent a week down here going over every scenario to get through these bars. What's your plan?"

"We need everyone's help," I said. "Ronark, what's our best bet?"

"We go after Rogers," he replied. All eyes turned toward him. "Think about it. Who's the one person Valkas trusts?"

"Um… Valkas," Andi stated like it was obvious.

Ronark sighed. "Besides himself. The only reasonable explanation I can think of for why we didn't find the dagger on him is because Rogers had it. He's the only person Valkas would entrust with it. It's not like Rogers can use it against him, and the guy would do anything to protect it."

"Are you sure?" I asked. Valkas didn't seem like he'd trust anyone.

"Valkas suspected you might come after him," Ronark pointed out. "But he wouldn't have expected you to go after Rogers."

"True," I agreed. "And even if I did, he wouldn't expect me to have a chance against him. Something on this island has been blocking my magic."

"It has to be Rogers," Ronark theorized. "He's cloaked the island from outsiders. I'm sure he can do something to limit another witch's magic, too."

Fiona and Teagan shared a wide-eyed glance.

"What?" Jenna asked. "What is it?"

"That would explain why Sondra had trouble with her magic when we got here," Fiona said. "But it only weakened her."

"Me, too," I said, thinking about the few times I'd gotten fire to rise from my palm.

"That's why they beat her to unconsciousness and put the spell over her," Teagan told us. "So she couldn't use her magic to get us out."

I pressed my lips together, thinking. "If Rogers can block witch magic, why not block shifter magic, too?"

"It probably affects the way we taste," Andi theorized.

Ronark nodded. "That, or they don't find it necessary. Rogers is only barely a high witch. His powers look impressive, but he has trouble maintaining them. He has the strength but not the endurance. He has to renew the spell cloaking the island every day, I know that much. A more powerful witch should be able to break down his spells."

"How do you know?" Andi asked.

Ronar smirked. "I've been around a long time, sweet cheeks."

"I thought only the witch who created a spell could break it," I said.

Ronark shrugged. "Depends on how powerful you are. Like I said, Rogers' magic is a little... touchy. His spells wouldn't last long after his death if he weren't around to maintain them."

"How would one break his spells?" I asked. "I mean, if I wanted to lift the spell that's keeping me from using my magic?"

Ronark breathed a heavy sigh. "Do you want the fast and easy solution or the slow and tough one?"

"Fast and easy," I answered automatically.

"You'd have to kill him."

Of course. I wasn't at all surprised.

"Okay," I said with a deep breath. "We'll get to Rogers, get the dagger, and then kill Valkas. Any objections?"

Teagan was the first to respond. "Ryland and I are in, but how are we getting out of here?"

"Is anyone good at picking locks?" Jenna asked.

Andi raised her hand. "I can."

"Perfect." Jenna turned to me with a smile. "Rach, your corset. It can get us out of here."

I glanced down at my dress in realization. Valkas could mock me all he wanted, but it was our ticket out of here. I reached for the bottom of my corset and tore the fabric, then grabbed on to the wire boning and pulled it out. I handed the wire to Jenna, who passed it along to Ronark and then to Andi.

"Once we're all out, I'm going to stay here," Teagan announced.

"No, babe," Ryland disagreed immediately.

"I'm human," Teagan pointed out. "I don't have the strength that the rest of you have, and I don't have my knives on me. There are hundreds of vampires up there. I would rather stay and make sure that no one comes down here and harms Sondra."

A weight settled in my gut when I glanced to Sondra. I could see her chest rising and falling; otherwise, she hadn't moved since I'd arrived. I didn't want anything to happen to her, either.

"I think Teagan has a point," I said. "Sondra can't come with us. If someone comes down here to see we're gone, they might hurt her even more."

"I'm with you, Teagan," Ryland said.

"But we need you," Fiona objected. "You're the biggest, strongest shifter here."

Ryland smirked. "Thanks for the vote, sis, but I'm not leaving Teagan and Sondra alone. In fact, I have a better idea. We'll head for the boathouse we saw when we came in. We'll get a boat ready in case all hell breaks loose."

Ronark checked an imaginary watch on his wrist. "By my estimate, the Awakening Ball is still going on. Security at the boathouse should be pretty thin."

"That's fine," I said to Ryland. "We don't want to be seen, so we should start with a small group anyway."

"Well, I'm going with Rae," Fiona insisted.

"Me, too," Jenna chimed in.

"I'm not breaking us out of here just to stay down here," Andi said as the lock on her cell disengaged. She quickly rushed out of the door and started on Ronark's lock.

"If anyone's going after the vampires, it's me," Ronark stated.

"Yeah, we need you," I replied. "You know this place better than any of us."

"Where will we find Rogers?" Jenna asked Ronark as Andi started fiddling with the lock on her cell.

Ronark stepped out of his open cell. "Rogers is part of Valkas's security team, so he should be monitoring the perimeter of the ballroom. We should have no problem getting to him."

Andi finished with the lock on my door and turned to Fiona's cell. I rushed out of my cell and stood outside Venn's. Seeing him lying on the floor, shivering in pain, sent another wave of emotions to rise within me. I placed my hand over my face and steadied myself against the wall. My breath wavered, and a hot tear streaked my cheek.

"What are we going to do about Venn?" I asked in a shaky tone.

Andi finished the lock on Fiona's cell and started on the next one.

Fiona stepped forward to place a comforting hand on my shoulder. "I don't know if there's anything we *can* do for him anymore."

An involuntary sob broke out in my chest. I knew it was true. It was just hard to hear it said out loud. I couldn't stand the thought of just leaving him.

"I know how hard this is." Fiona's voice cracked. "I don't want to say goodbye to him, either."

I reached for the bars of his cell and lowered myself to my knees. I felt another hand rest on my back to join Fiona's and tilted my head up to see Jenna at my side.

I looked back to Venn, my heart breaking all over again. His back moved quickly to the beat of his breath.

"It's like watching him slowly die right in front of me," I whispered.

A sudden, horrible thought occurred to me to put him out of his misery, but I knew I'd ever be able to go through with it. The only thing I could do was kill Valkas. And with him, Venn would perish as well.

I couldn't bear to think about it like that, as if Valkas and Venn were connected as one. It made me sick.

"Venn." My soft whisper cut through the silence in the dungeons.

At the sound of his voice, Venn's breathing slowed, and my heart lifted. Was he still in there somewhere?

"Venn?" I said in a stronger voice this time.

He lifted his head, and it was like another shot straight through the heart. His eyes looked straight through me. Silver eyes. Not Venn's deep brown eyes I loved so much. It was like he was already gone.

I took a breath to calm my racing heart, but no amount of deep breathing or relaxation exercises could calm me right now. The love of my life was withering away before me, and I felt as if my heart was crumbling right along with him. This couldn't be the end for us.

But it was. In this life, it was. And if his soul was damned, then we'd never live another life together. I barely had any time with him. I'd give anything for just a few more moments.

"Rae."

A sharp breath crossed my lips as Venn spoke my name.

"Venn, are you still there?" I asked desperately. "I'm so sorry. You don't deserve this."

He pushed himself to a sitting position, and I thought for a second that I saw a light cross his eyes. I reached out for him, but Jenna pulled me back the same time Venn shied away into the corner of his cell. He curled his knees to his chest and turned his face away from me, like he was ashamed.

"You can't save everyone, Rae," he whispered so lightly that I barely heard him.

"Venn…"

He looked at me again, but his eyelids twitched, like it was difficult to meet my gaze—like it pained him. "Fiona's right. You can't help me anymore. The venom…" He gritted his teeth and sucked a deep breath.

My eyes went wide. Venn bit his lower lip, and I noticed for the first time his canines seemed longer than normal. Tears rushed down my face faster.

Venn forced the words out through shaky breaths. "The venom has already done too much damage. I can already feel the bloodlust setting in. I'm a danger to all of you now."

"You just hold on," I told him, but I didn't know what for. I didn't have a solution to this. And that ached to the very core of my soul.

Venn scooted himself closer to me, eyeing my fingers around the bars. I bit down hard on the inside of my lip to keep from bawling like a child. He was just within reach, yet so far away.

"You have to go, Rae," Venn said softly, looking me in the eyes. "I don't want you to see me like this."

"But Venn, we don't have long before—"

"Exactly," he cut me off. "We don't have long. You need to go get that dagger."

"He's right," Ronark cut in. "Someone's bound to come check on us at some point."

Fiona wiped at her eyes, then reached for my hand, but I pulled away from her. Venn was so close to me now, and I wasn't missing my chance to give him a proper goodbye.

Goodbye. This couldn't be it, could it? I wasn't willing to believe that… yet deep down in my heart, I couldn't deny it.

"Venn." I squeezed my eyes shut, letting the tears stream down my face. Without thinking about it too hard, I reached through the bars, grabbed on to him, and pulled him toward me. "I love you."

My mouth connected with his. It felt like kissing him for the first time. Fireworks went off in my chest, and a sense of peace surged through me. Yet it felt so comfortable, like we'd done this a thousand times before.

A split second later, his teeth clamped around my lower lip. Pain shot through my mouth, and the taste of copper rushed over my tongue. I screamed. Suddenly, at least three pairs of hands were on me, dragging me backward.

I forgot all about the blood in my mouth as Venn threw his head backwards and groaned in agony. Muscles rippled across his chest, like there was a power trying to escape out of his skin.

"Go," he forced between clenched teeth. "I. Can't. Control…"

Ronark dragged me to my feet. "We need to finish this."

Venn's heavy breaths filled the dungeon. He leaned forward and rested on his palms. He lifted his head, and I could just barely see the last bits of the Venn I knew staring out at me through those silver eyes.

"Go, Rae," he whispered. "And know that I will *never* stop loving you."

"I love you, too," I called back as Jenna and Fiona began leading me down the hall. Teagan and Ryland turned to Sondra's cell, and I added, "We'll see you soon."

We raced down the hall and turned toward the stairs. Just before we reached the end, Jenna grabbed my shoulder and stopped me. She threw her arms around me and squeezed me tight. Ronark, Andi, and Fiona all stopped to wait for us.

"I'm so sorry about Venn," Jenna said.

I hugged her back, but it didn't feel like I could squeeze hard enough to show her how much I appreciated the thought.

"Thank you," I said before drawing away.

My eyes fell on Fiona's sad expression, and I gestured for her to join us. Fiona stepped forward, and I wrapped an arm around her as she wiped the last remaining tears out of her eyes.

"I love you guys," I said.

"We love you, too," Fiona replied.

Finally, I drew away from them and stood up straighter. I'd cried just about as many tears as I possibly could, and my eyes had gone dry. I swallowed down the lump in my throat and took a breath. "Let's go slay some vampires."

21

Music from the ballroom spilled out from open doorways when we reached the top of the stairs. Quietly, we snuck out into the hallway. Ronark led us down a narrow hall and peeked around the corner. He threw his arm out across Andi's chest and pressed her back to the wall. The rest of us followed suit. I held my breath and forced my heart rate to slow.

Ronark placed an index finger over his lips, then peeked out around the corner again. Silently, he gestured for us to follow.

Halfway down the hall, we heard a pair of footsteps approaching. Ronark shoved us into a dark room. Judging by the shapes I could just barely make out through the darkness, it looked like some sort of study. Ronark stood at the door and peered through the sliver into the hallway until the sound of footsteps disappeared.

"Come on," Ronark hissed, leading us back out into the hall.

Fiona kept close to my side, her eyes darting this way and

that. As we stopped the end of the hall, a collection of voices reached us.

"He's bluffing," a man accused.

"Am I?" another challenged.

"Just fold already." I recognized Rogers's voice.

"Poker?" I whispered in disbelief. Valkas was hosting the celebration of the year, and his security team was out here playing poker.

Ronark shrugged. "Makes things easy for us."

He looked around the corner, and I poked my head out beside him. I saw that we were in the hallway that led to the big sitting area with the large arches and the grand piano. Four guys sat around the couches with cards in their hands.

"What do we do?" Andi asked. "I can create a distraction if you need it."

"I think we can take them," I said. "It's one human and three vampires against five shifters."

"No, no," Ronark replied. "I think Andi's right. A distraction will give us a better advantage. They're less powerful if we split them up."

"So are we," Jenna pointed out.

"Jenna's right," Andi whispered. "We'll take them all at once. But we have only one shot to catch them off guard. I'm going to distract them, so get ready to strike."

Ronark turned to me and grabbed on to my shoulders, staring me in the eyes. "You take Rogers, Rachel. He's not as powerful as he seems. You can break through his spells. I know you can."

"You've never seen me perform magic," I pointed out.

"Doesn't matter. Every witch has something worth fighting for. Just make sure your reason is stronger than his."

I nodded.

"That a girl." Ronark patted my back, then turned to Andi. He dragged her into a hug and placed a kiss on the top of her head. "Be careful, baby doll."

"I will."

"What's the signal?" Fiona asked.

"You'll know." Andi winked.

Andi padded softly down the hall in her jaguar form, not making a single noise. She kept close to the wall and ducked under tables and around other decor to keep from being seen.

When she reached the first wide archway, she waited until she saw all the men had their eyes on their cards before hopping forward silently and ducking behind a couch.

Rogers glanced up from his cards and looked out into the hallway. He went rigid, as if he was on high alert. I could barely see him from this angle, but he seemed to relax a moment later and looked back down at his cards.

Andi lowered herself onto her belly and slid along the hardwood floor, her fur helping to muffle the noise. She cocked her head at us just before disappearing out of view.

Ronark led the way, sneaking out into the wide hallway as we all followed behind him. We kept close to the wall where the vampires couldn't see us, then stopped just before we reached the first arch. We were only mere feet away from the couches.

"Full house," a vampire with a bald head announced.

Just then, the sound of the piano filled the hall. It was a soft, beautiful melody. All four of the security guards' eyes widened as they looked to the corner of the room where Andi was playing. Three of the men—all but Rogers—shot to their feet.

"Hey!" Baldy called. "What are you—?"

"Now!" Ronark hissed.

The four of us jumped out at them while they were momentarily distracted by Andi's music. Ronark shifted and slammed into one of the vamps facing away from us. Fiona took the other, while Jenna jumped on the arm of the couch and kicked off, using her momentum to soar over the other two guys. She shifted mid-air and landed in raccoon form on Baldy's shiny head.

Meanwhile, I went for Rogers. I aimed straight for his eyes, but it was like he knew I was coming. He swung his arm out, and it connected with my chest so hard that when I gasped, no air came. My body flew across the room and slammed into the small section of wall between the archways.

Holy hell! Rogers is strong. Way stronger than any human should be, I realized.

I pushed past the pain in my chest and jumped to my feet before Rogers could reach me. Andi had abandoned her act on the piano and had joined Jenna in wrestling her guy onto the couch. Fiona grabbed a plant and swung the heavy pot at one of the vamp's head.

"A shifter, huh?" I shot at Rogers.

"Valkas would only pick the very best for his team." He smirked before throwing a fist in my direction. I ducked, and his knuckles connected with the wall behind me, sending crumbled pieces flying everywhere.

I kicked my leg out at him, and it sank into his abdomen. He let out a satisfying grunt, but it barely fazed him. He grabbed for me and caught me by the wrist, then spun me around until I was pinned to his chest.

"What's in it for you?" I asked. "Money? Fame?"

Rogers scoffed. "None of your business. How'd you get out of your cell?"

"None of your business," I shot back at him. I threw my

arms downward with all my strength, breaking free of his hold. I dove toward a vase on the end table to use as a weapon and held it above my head.

But before I could bring it down on him, he muttered the words, "*Quod dico facies.*"

My whole body stopped as if I'd been turned to stone, but my eyes still moved freely. I glanced over to my friends to see that Fiona had taken care of the first guy was helping Ronark with his. Any second now, they'd come to help me, too. Come hell or high water, we were getting our hands on that dagger.

Rogers stepped closer to me until his face was just inches from my own. "If you must know, I want to be on the winning side."

"You sure you chose the right one?" I asked rhetorically.

Rogers reached down and clamped a hand around my jaw. When he touched me, something like a small electric shot traveled across my skin. It was like I could feel his magic in his touch, and I knew that everything Ronark had said about him was true. Rogers's magic was strong, but it was without purpose. He was driven by fear and greed, and that was why he had to renew his cloaking spell every day. His magic was weak.

"Valkas is stronger than any witch alive," Rogers asserted. "You're the only thing standing in his way of eternal glory. And *I'm* stronger than you. Together, Valkas and I can rule the world."

"And what about when you die?" I asked. "If you become a vampire to live forever, you'll lose your magic. You don't think Valkas will toss you aside the second you're no use to him?"

Rogers hesitated to answer the question.

"Besides, if you're so strong, how come your spell stopped working on me a good ten seconds ago?"

Rogers's eyes went wide and darted up to the vase I held above his head. I'd been totally bluffing, but the second I said it, he lost his focus. His spell eased on me just enough that I found control over my fingers again. I opened my hand, and the heavy vase clunked into his forehead.

He was barely distracted for a second, but it was enough. I brought my knee up and pressed my foot firmly into his abdomen, then kicked with all my strength. He went flying backward and crashed into a table next to the couches. It crumbled beneath his weight. I was on him a second later, patting him down in search of the dagger.

His arms shot out and grabbed on to my wrists, so I threw my head forward into his nose. My head throbbed, but I was satisfied to see blood dripping down his face and onto the hardwood floor. Still, he didn't let go of me.

I pulled a move I'd seen in a movie once. I threw my arms outward, giving me enough momentum to break his hold on me. I grabbed his wrists with all my strength and tugged so that they crossed over his chest. I pressed my knee right where his arms met and again felt around for the dagger.

Relief flooded through me when my hands ran over a sheath secured to his hip. I pulled hard on his suitcoat, tearing the buttons and a corner of fabric.

I'll be damned. Ronark was right. Beneath the fabric of his coat, the silver handle of the dagger poked out of the sheath.

The moment I reached for it, Rogers let out a deep, angry roar from beneath me. He gathered all his strength and threw his arms out, tossing me off of him like a rag doll. My cheek slammed into the corner of the couch several feet away, but I ignored the pulse of pain and whirled around.

Rogers was already coming at me again, his fist flying at my face. I ducked, but I didn't get out of the way in time before a pain shot out through my other cheek. I stumbled backwards into another end table. I grabbed the legs and held the whole thing high above my head, swinging it at Rogers.

He threw his arm up to protect himself. The table snapped in half against his forearm, and the legs went flying in different directions. I was left with two legs in my hands and half a table top. So I swung it again.

This time, Rogers caught it mid-swing and twisted, ripping it out of my hands. I didn't let myself get distracted. Jumping onto the arm of the couch, I kicked off to gain height, then twisted in the air to land on Rogers's back. I curled my arm around his neck and squeezed tightly, but he was just as fast as I was. He grabbed on to my arm and threw his body forward, using the momentum to flip me over his head and slam me onto my back on the ground.

The air stalled in my lungs like the whole room had just been sucked of oxygen.

"You think you're so tough," Rogers drawled as he loomed above me. "You will *never* amount to anything as long as the Soulless are around."

I finally caught my breath and managed to choke out, "We'll see about that."

In a split second, I kicked off the ground, spun and grabbed the dagger out of Rogers's sheath, then sliced the hand racing for my throat. I jumped backward just out of his reach. My ankle met up with the wall behind me, and I held out the dagger in defense.

Anger ignited across his eyes, and his nostrils flared. He aimed his good fist at me, but I easily ducked and dodged it. What I didn't expect was for him to go straight for the sconce behind me, ripping it off the wall. Before I could react, a hot, burning pain seared my shoulder as he shoved the burning candle into my exposed skin.

My scream echoed above the breaking glass and grunts coming from the other side of the room. Rogers took the opportunity to reach down and tear the dagger out of my grasp.

That was it before he made a run for it.

"Rachel!" I heard Jenna calling my name, but I didn't listen. No way was I letting Rogers get away with that dagger.

I sprinted after him, down one hall and around a corner, until we reached a back door and broke out into the night. I ran after him as fast as I could, but he kept a steady pace ahead of me. He raced around the chateau and to a familiar trail, the one that led to the fight ring. My chest ached with shallow breaths the harder I pushed my body to keep up with him.

What the hell is he up to?

Rogers didn't slow until he reached the arena at the top of the hill. When I finally caught up to him, he was standing at the edge of the cliff, dangling the dagger over the water.

Dread slammed into my gut so hard that the air *whooshed* out of my lungs. I stopped in my tracks. It felt like I'd been punched in the stomach by Thor's hammer.

"Don't!" I cried, holding my hands out in front of me, as if I could reason with him.

But there was no reasoning with the Soulless. He'd already made his decision.

Rogers opened his fingers, and the dagger dropped out of sight. All of my hope fell with it, crashing into the waves below.

Instinctively, I shifted and flapped my wings, as if I might be able to catch it before it hit the water. But my wings failed to lift me into the air. I'd almost forgotten Valkas had ripped out my flight feathers. I shifted back to human form, feeling completely hopeless.

Maybe if I had a spell to stop it, or something to drag it up from the deep lake bed below… But I didn't have any of that. All I had was tonight, and my final chance had vanished in the blink of an eye.

Before I could really process what had just happened, Rogers's features started changing. His head ballooned as his body grew hundreds of pounds heavier. His skin transformed into a dark gray color, and it looked dry and rough. His nose elongated into a long, sharp horn.

A rhino! He was a freaking rhino shifter.

I quickly glanced around for a weapon and spotted a sharp rock at my feet. I knelt down and curled my fingers around the cool stone. My mind raced with possible solutions. A sharp rock against a rhino didn't give me the best odds. I needed magic.

Ronark's words instantly came back to me. *Every witch has something worth fighting for. Just make sure your reason is stronger than his.*

Rogers scuffed his foot in the dirt and lowered his head, aiming his horn at me. But for whatever reason, it didn't ignite a sense of fear within me like it should've. I remained calm.

As Rogers stood there threatening me, I turned my focus inward. I felt for the magic I knew was there, but instead of digging deep into my own magic, I searched for the barrier Rogers had placed over the island. My magic slammed against an imaginary brick wall. I pictured my magic spreading out across it, looking for weaknesses in the spell.

"Want to know the difference between you and me?" I asked boldly.

Rogers tilted his head to the side, like I'd piqued his curiosity.

"I have a family worth fighting for," I said.

This one's for you guys.

Rogers huffed and took aim, sprinting for me like he was going to impale me through the heart. But I raised my hand in defense.

Suddenly, my magic tore through the wall like a stick of dynamite blasting through brick. All at once, the power inside of me that had been held back erupted out of my palms. Air blasted backward with the power of a hurricane, leaving me safely in the eye of the storm. The bleachers crumbled, and trees bowed over as Rogers's body flew backwards at the force of my magic. He tumbled through the sky over and over, letting out a terrified whine. Then he was gone, thrust over the side of a cliff toward the rocks below.

In the blink of an eye, the storm was over. Trees righted themselves, and silence settled over the arena. It was almost like it hadn't happened at all. I stood there for a moment, dumbstruck. All that power… and I hadn't even muttered an incantation?

The sound of distant screams reached my ears, bringing me back to attention. I looked out over the trees toward the chateau, and my hand shot over my mouth. From this vantage point, I could see into the tall, wide windows that lined the ballroom. All throughout the room, blood slaves had shifted and vampires were going wild. The entirety of the island had turned on the Soulless. The sound of shattering glass was barely audible in the distance as two shifters threw a vampire through a window and glass rained down around him.

This isn't over yet, I realized. My family needed me.

I started toward the trail, knowing that I had to get down there and help them. But just as I reached the trees, a tall, dark figure stepped out of the shadows, blocking my path. My heart leapt my chest.

"Well, well, well," a voice came from out of the darkness. "You really should've stayed in your cell, darling."

My blood ran cold as the figure stepped out of the trees and into the moonlight.

Valkas had come for me. Judging by the evil sneer on his face, he was finally done playing games.

22

"How does it feel?" Valkas mocked, taking another step into the arena. "Knowing this is finally the end? Without that dagger, you'll never kill me, not unless you dive into the lake to retrieve it. The rocks at the bottom will kill you first." He smirked in satisfaction.

"There are other ways to stop you," I said confidently.

"How's that?" He feigned interest. "Trapping me on this island again? Darling, you don't have the manpower. Besides, look at how well that worked out last time." He gestured to himself, like he was living proof that my magic was weak.

The honest truth was that I didn't know how to stop him. I didn't even know how to slow him down.

Valkas took another step toward me and reached out to brush my hair over my shoulder, exposing my neck.

I slapped his hand away. In my other hand, my grip tightened on the rock I'd been holding. "Don't touch me."

"Darling," he snarled, leaning in close. His breath brushed across my face, sending shivers through my cheek. "I own you."

The next moment passed in the blink of an eye, but I saw it as if it were in slow motion. Valkas's hands shot out to wrap around me as his fangs elongated and headed toward my neck. He threw my body backward like we were a couple dancing on the clifftop and he was dipping me romantically. But there was nothing romantic about the moment.

As I felt the ground swoop out from under me, I shoved my rock upward—straight into his ribs. It was a last resort, one that I thought might slow him down... but it didn't.

Valkas's teeth sank into my neck, sending a needle-sharp pain across my skin. A split second later, that peaceful euphoria set in. Somewhere in the back of my mind, I knew this was not something to enjoy. This was a sign of the end.

I stared up at the night sky as strong emotions welled to the surface, overpowering that feeling Valkas's bite gave me. For so many years, anger and frustration were all I knew. But this was different. It was heavier. The weight pulling on my chest was full of regret and sorrow. Somewhere along the way, everything had fallen to pieces, and it pained me to the very core to know that I wouldn't get a chance to make things right again.

I thought of Venn, withering away to nothing in that cell. I thought of Sondra, how she'd been beaten to unconsciousness because of me. Jenna, how she'd been kidnapped and kept prisoner here all these years. Fiona, Teagan, Ryland, Ronark, Andi... all the other blood slaves on this island.

I'd come here to save them. And I didn't.

As I thought of them, one thought broke through all the others.

At least they knew I loved them.

The weight in my chest eased at the thought, and a sense

of peace washed over me. It wasn't from Valkas's bite, either. This peace came from inside of me.

At least if nothing else came of this, my family knew I loved them. Maybe I wouldn't kill Valkas, and maybe the vampires would live on. They could take this world from us, destroy everything we held dear and rule as they had planned. But they would never take the moments. They would never take the feelings. They would never take *us*.

It was in that moment that I realized with unwavering certainty that Jenna was right. The Soulless couldn't break me unless I let them.

At the thought, a power rose within me, a strong tingling of magic I'd never felt before. It was unlike the fire or the lightning I'd conjured in the past. This magic was hundreds of times stronger, like a nuclear bomb about to go off inside my body.

Love, I realized. This was what it was like to love someone with so much passion that you thought your heart might explode.

You should know that there's always more than one way off an island. That's what Genevieve had said. I didn't know why those words came back to me in that moment, but I knew it meant something. Only... what?

Was she talking about the island in a literal sense, or was it a metaphor? And if it was a metaphor, then what did it mean?

A red-hot, searing pain entered my veins as Valkas released his venom. It felt as if someone had placed burning hot coals on my neck, turning my blood to flames. My body went completely rigid, and I longed to scream, but the cry of agony caught in my throat, unable to escape.

And that was when Genevieve's meaning hit me.

Even when strong bridges crumble, there's always another path to take.

She meant it as a mental island, the feeling of being stuck, alone, and hopeless. *The feeling of no escape.*

She was trying to tell me that magic had loopholes, that even though I'd lost the dagger, there were other ways to break the vampire curse. That had to be it.

I struggled through the pain clouding my thoughts, trying to think of what I knew about magic. A curse like this could only be broken by the witch who cast it through an object used in the original spell.

The dagger wasn't the only thing there when the spell was cast, I suddenly realized. I recalled the vision I'd had of Valkas, how I'd sliced his hand open with the dagger and watched his blood stream into a bowl.

It took everything I had to force words out between clenched teeth. "*Quod. Dico. Facies.*"

At my command, Valkas went rigid. I could barely sense it over the searing venom pulsing through my body, but I saw his muscles stiffen as I spoke the incantation for the puppeteer spell I'd seen Rogers use.

Drop me, I commanded in my mind.

Suddenly, my body fell from his grasp, and I landed hard in the dirt at his feet. Valkas stood above me with wide eyes filled with fright. He otherwise looked like a statue.

I pointed my hand at him and forced him to stand straight up. Blood dripped out of his open mouth. I could see in his eyes he was struggling to close his lips, but he couldn't.

I got to my feet. I pressed one hand against the wound on my neck and kept the other pointed at him. Rage burned behind his motionless eyes. I quickly whispered the incantation for healing, then wiped the blood from my neck.

"I remember slitting your palm," I said. "The dagger was the obvious option, but it never was the only one, was it?"

Valkas's eyes grew wider the more I talked.

"All I need to break this spell is something used when the spell was created. The dagger isn't the only weapon that can kill you. You, Valkas, were there," I stated as it became clear to me what I needed to do. "Which means you're a weapon against yourself."

I forced him to pull the sharp rock from his side, then let him take control of his mouth again. His scream echoed over the cliffside like a creature howling at the moon. He brought the rock to his chest under my command. Images of all the terrible things I'd seen the Soulless do flashed through my mind, but I settled on just one…

The day I came here, when Valkas had ripped that man's heart from his chest. After all the horrible things he'd done, Valkas deserved to know what it felt like to be one of his own victims.

"Stop it, Rachel!" he shouted. "You don't underst —GAHHH!"

I made him press the rock into his skin. It tore through his flesh and scraped along the bone like a blade cutting through ice. It carved out a deep, long wound surrounded by raw skin running from his collarbone all the way down to his sternum. Nausea hit me at the sight of it, but I forced the bile down my throat to concentrate.

Valkas screamed like I'd never heard anyone scream before. The sound of his voice carried over the empty water like a banshee in the night.

Drop the rock, I commanded in my mind.

He did, still screaming like he couldn't bear the pain any longer.

By the simple twitch of my finger, Valkas shoved his hand into his open chest cavity. He removed it a moment later and held up a dry, black heart.

His features contorted in a mix between disgust, fury, and terror. "You evil bit—"

The vengeance I felt toward Valkas melted away. This wasn't about revenge anymore. This was about saving the people I loved.

I curled my hand into a tight fist, forcing him to do the same. Valkas squeezed as hard as he possibly could.

It was ironic. The same hand that gave blood to create him would be the same to destroy him.

"*Biiiiitch!*" he roared.

The heart turned to ash in his hand.

I released my hold on him as the ashes drifted away in the wind. Valkas gasped and took a step toward me, but his legs began to crumble beneath him. He fell to the ground, and I watched in peaceful satisfaction as the spell broke before my very eyes. Valkas reached a hand out toward me, but his fingers washed away in the wind like sand upon a beach.

He shot me one last pleading look, as if begging me to reverse the spell, to keep him alive. But I could see it in his eyes—he already knew it was over.

"How does it feel?" I asked calmly, throwing his words back at him. "Knowing this is finally the end?"

He gaped at me as his body crumbled away. It took his arms and legs first, then his body, before finally wiping away the wide-eyed expression on his face. And then he was just... gone.

Valkas's clothes remained in a pile at my feet.

The pain of the venom rushing through my veins eased as the vampire curse broke. Relief so strong washed through me like a tidal wave hitting shore. Tears sprang to my eyes before I even knew they were coming and streamed down my face.

My whole body shivered, and I dropped to my hands and knees, curling up into a ball with my forehead pressed to the grass. Deep breaths passed in and out of my lungs as I tried to regain my physical strength and process what had just happened. I couldn't believe it.

Never again would I give up, no matter how bad the situation. Tonight proved to me that anything was possible.

Against all odds, I had finally beat Valkas.

23

"Rachel!" The sound of Jenna's voice carried through the trees and over the cliff.

I didn't know how long I'd been kneeling there, staring down at Valkas's empty shirt, unable to believe he was truly gone. Eight years ago, he'd escaped from this island and the whole world changed. Now things could go back to normal.

I didn't even know what that looked like anymore. It felt like magic had been part of the world my whole life.

Magic. We still had magic. Of course things wouldn't go back to the way they were. Witches and shifters were still out in the open. But maybe now that the vampire curse was broken, magic wouldn't be so feared. We could embrace it, give it a different face than the horror vampires had put to it. We could use it for good.

"Rachel!" Jenna's voice came again, pulling me out of my thoughts.

"Rae!" Fiona's voice quickly followed.

"Up here!" I called.

"Rachel, oh my God." Jenna rushed out of the trees and fell to her knees beside me. She lightly reached out to touch the tender bruises on my face, but she pulled away at the last second. "What happened?"

"I... I killed him," I said, glancing between Fiona and Jenna. They were banged up and bruised themselves, but I didn't notice any major injuries. "I killed Valkas." I wasn't sure I truly believed it until I said the words out loud. "What about you? Did Ronark and Andi make it?"

Jenna dropped her gaze. "We fought off the vampires in the hall, but when we tried following you, we lost you in the chateau. We thought Rogers had led you to the ballroom. Only... when we got there, you weren't there."

"A fight broke out," Fiona said. "Before we knew it, all the blood slaves had joined us—shifters, human, all of them."

"Are Ronark and Andi okay?" I repeated.

Jenna took a long breath. "Andi didn't make it. A vampire got ahold of her—"

"I don't want to know how it happened," I interrupted.

Jenna nodded in understanding. "Ronark is fine. He's leading everyone in rounding up the Soulless."

I instantly became more alert. I lifted my gaze and looked down the hill toward the chateau. Windows were smashed, and bodies were strewn here and there. From what I could see through the windows, people walked slowly. Everything seemed so quiet and somber compared to when I'd seen the place in an uproar earlier.

"You mean, the vampires aren't dead?" I asked. When I killed Valkas, all the vampires should've died with him. The magic keeping them alive should've disappeared. "I thought I broke the vampire curse."

Fiona shot a glance at Jenna, like she didn't know how to tell me what came next. She placed a gentle hand on my shoulder and said, "You did. They just didn't die."

"What do you mean?" I asked, bewildered. "What happened?"

"It happened all of a sudden," Jenna explained. "We were losing people left and right, then suddenly... we just weren't. It was like the vampires lost their strength. We started winning, and they began surrendering."

"We all kind of realized what was happening at the same time," Fiona said. "The silver faded from their eyes, and..."

"You mean they're human again?" It didn't seem possible.

Jenna nodded. "Yes. It doesn't excuse their crimes, but—"

Before Jenna could finish, a shot of adrenaline jolted through my chest. I sprang to my feet so fast I nearly lost my balance. I clutched on to Jenna's and Fiona's shoulders to steady myself. "Oh my God! Do you know what this means?" I didn't wait for their response before answering my own question. "Venn!"

I sprinted down the trail and back toward the chateau. Fiona and Jenna were close at my heels. Inside, we navigated through an endless labyrinth of hallways until we found the door leading to the dungeons. I ran down them so fast that I almost lost my footing and slid all the way down. I caught myself on the railing and didn't stop running until we reached the cells.

I skidded to a halt to take in the scene. Teagan and Ryland were long gone, and Sondra's shackles hung empty. The wire used to pick the locks lay on the ground beside them. Venn stood with his hands on the bars of his cell, looking like it took all his strength to stay upright. His soft brown eyes met mine, and relief flooded through me. Venn looked down at himself in confusion. It was like he couldn't process what was going on.

"Venn!" I rushed over to him, grabbed the wire, and began fiddling with the lock on his cell. My fingers shook so badly that I couldn't get it in the hole.

"What happened?" Venn asked, sounding a bit disoriented.

Jenna grabbed the wire from me and began working on the lock so I could focus on Venn.

I reached out to take his hands. "I did it, Venn. I killed Valkas."

He looked beyond relieved. "How did I survive? The transformation must've not finished."

I shook my head, choking back the tears. "No, it only killed Valkas. Everyone else survived, but the spell is broken now."

The lock clicked free on Venn's cell. I yanked the door open and fell into his arms.

"I thought I'd lost you," I whispered.

His lips met mine, and I knew without a doubt. It was Venn—my Venn. Valkas had failed to take him from me.

My chest came alive, sending a rush of happiness through my veins like a strong ocean current whipping me off my feet and pulling me out to sea. I'd never felt such an emotion hit me so fast and so strong before. He cupped the sides of my face and tilted my head back. His tongue slipped inside my mouth, sending that ocean current to take me faster.

He drew away and spoke through shallow breaths. "I thought so, too. I'm glad everyone's okay."

I relaxed into him for a mere moment, until I remembered Sondra was still hurt. Now that Rogers was dead, she'd be waking any moment—if she wasn't awake already.

"Sondra," I said quickly.

Fiona gave me a wide-eyed look, like she just realized something. "Your magic's working. You can heal her!"

"Then let's go," Jenna insisted.

Venn took my hand, and the four of us hurried out of the chateau and to the boathouse. When we arrived, we found Teagan and Ryland preparing an expensive-looking boat for the journey home. It looked even fancier than the one Richard had brought me there on. The boathouse itself was just as nice as the chateau, with three stalls for different sized boats. It looked like a fancy garage, only with docks for flooring and open water where the boats sat. Several piles of clothes covered in ashes lined the dock, presumably where Ryland and Teagan had killed the boathouse guards.

"Nothing's going to happen to them," Teagan was saying to Ryland. "They'll be fine—oh my God!" She caught sight of us and jumped off the boat onto the dock. "You're okay!"

Teagan stopped in her tracks when she noticed Venn with us. Slowly, she backed away. "What's going on?"

"Rae did it!" Fiona exclaimed. "She killed Valkas and broke the curse."

Teagan's eyebrows came together. "Vampires are... human again?"

"Apparently," Fiona answered, shooting a smile in Venn's direction.

"What happens to their souls?" Teagan asked. "I mean, are the Soulless still... soulless?"

"We're not sure yet," Jenna said. "Venn could be different since the transformation wasn't finished. All we know is the others are still alive."

Ryland poked his head out of the cabin. "If they're still a threat, then we have to go."

"I don't think they are," Jenna admitted. "The blood slaves

outnumber them, and they surrendered as soon as the spell broke."

"Let's heal Sondra," I suggested. "Then we can figure out how we're getting everyone off this island."

"This way." Ryland gestured to me to follow him.

We stepped inside the cabin to see Sondra lying across one of the bench seats. Her chest rose and fell slowly, but she otherwise didn't move. She looked so frail.

I knelt beside her and placed a gentle hand on her shoulder. Everyone went quiet while I took several long, deep breaths, trying to channel my power.

But the familiar tingle never came. That couldn't be, considering Rogers was dead and his spell had been broken. Had the fall not killed him? Was he still blocking my magic?

No, that didn't seem right. This seemed stronger… like my entire connection to Synchrony had been severed.

That's when it hit me.

Matias hadn't been misinformed about what would happen to the vampires when I broke the curse. He hadn't just taken a wild guess when he told me all vampires would perish with Valkas. He told me exactly what I wanted to hear— exactly what he knew would drive me toward this very ending.

"What's wrong?" Venn asked.

I looked up at my family in horror. "This was Matias's plan all along. There never was a successor. He wanted me to kill Valkas to release his own soul, so that he could access his witch magic again and use the Artifact. You guys…"

I could hardly breathe as the cold, dark reality of what had just happened hit me. "I played right into Matias's hands. And now he's taken all our magic."

END OF BOOK THREE

Continue the series in book four, *Retribute*.

ABOUT THE AUTHOR

Alicia Rades is a USA Today bestselling author of young adult and new adult paranormal fiction. When she's not dreaming up magical stories, she's either binge-watching paranormal TV shows, meditating, or spending time with her family. She has an unhealthy obsession with psychic characters and writes with a deck of tarot cards next to her computer.